# WEDNESDAY
## She took my heart away

### Part Three
### Life is what you make it

**K. Harder**

First Edition Design Publishing
Sarasota, Florida USA

Wednesday
Copyright ©2021, 2024  K. Harder

ISBN 978-1506-912-17-2 PBK
ISBN 978-1506-910-15-4 EBK

LCCN 2021900860

February 2021, 2024

Published and Distributed by
First Edition Design Publishing, Inc.
P.O. Box 17646, Sarasota, FL 34276-3217
www.firsteditiondesignpublishing.com

# The Second Battle of Lonesome Planet

One more time we approached Lonesome Planet. This time we silently entered into high orbit – carefully and very slowly. But we had nothing to worry about; everything was quiet. It almost looked too good to be true.

As I had anticipated, the biggest immediate threat - the two military spaceships - seemed to have returned to their home base.

Sitting in the main control room, I watched as the object of my desire came closer. It seemed so near that I could almost reach out and touch it.

This was the third time I arrived at Draco, the Lonesome Planet.

I was present at the first expedition where we lost everything and my beloved wife was killed by the enemy. This time, on our second expedition, our arrival had coincided with the arrival of the enemy. We had to retreat, but only temporarily.

Now we were back, ready to do our best.

But, unfortunately, this time the scenario from the first expedition repeated itself.

We attacked the enemy on the planet below with everything we had. This time around we were much better armed. But we no longer had the element of surprise.

To make matters worse, the enemy also seemed to have upgraded their military skills. Having tried it all once before, they handled the situation much better than we had expected.

It soon became obvious that we could not enter the planet's atmosphere. Every time we tried to establish a foothold on the surface the enemy fired rapid volleys of pure, destructive energy that would rip apart any incoming object long before it could make a successful landing.

We retaliated, dropping bombs big enough to blast small moons out of orbit. It made no difference. Both of their domes stubbornly stayed intact, as if they were mocking us for even trying.

But on the other hand, they were not able to attack us in outer space.

So we stayed in orbit.

In the end I did exactly the same thing that my late wife had resorted to. I placed my ship high above the smaller dome and rained down upon it a hellish, continuous beam of solar energy - enhanced and concentrated by our advanced laser technology.

It had no effect whatsoever.

I stubbornly continued the attack in the vain hope that sooner or later maybe they would suffer some kind of supply shortage that would finally make the enemy vulnerable.

And all the while I was worried sick. What if the catastrophe that had befallen my wife would repeat itself? Would our expedition be next in line to be wiped out?

I did not even know what had happened to my wife's small fleet of ships back then. When my wife ordered me to go home, I took my leave of that first and fatal expedition - and now, as a consequence of my ignorance, there was nothing I could do, no preparations I could make.

While Lonesome Planet slowly turned around its star, I relentlessly tried to pry open her defenses.

In the end I even used precious resources to construct external solar power installations in space. In this way I could keep the beam going even when it was black night on the planet's surface.

Seeing the beam touching the dome late at night was quite a sight to behold. It was a grand spectacle, much like fireworks, going down instead of up. But it was utterly unsuccessful.

The dome remained intact.

Apart from this failure, I had a fairly good time. I experienced none of the psychological problems that had haunted me so badly during the earlier phases of this expedition. Nobody questioned my leadership and I had a huge pile of tasks to keep myself busy. Walking down long and desolate spaceship corridors, I was able to turn corners without any fear of seeing the ghost of my wife.

Whenever I had the time, I would go sit in the Captain's seat in front of the big monitor, quietly looking at the wonderful planet down below. Later, in my lonely room, I would listen to JaNine's blue song about the starlight that shines on Lonesome Planet.

*This is the sequel to 'Like Cat And Dog' in 'Tuesday'. Long ago settlers arrived at the Beni planet, but they never noticed that someone was already there. These original inhabitants may not be corporeal as we understand it, but they are adept at manipulating their surroundings. They liked the newcomers to such a degree that they totally integrated with them.*

# Break Point

**Morgan Kade** looked gloomily down the endless row of grey and tan houses that lined the Pittarn on both sides. Today he had finished work early. Now he was on his way home. But on this particular day he did not feel like going home at all. Even on a nice day like this, his modest apartment on the outskirts of town would be just as bleak and empty as it had always seemed to be. When he arrived, nobody would be waiting there for him.

The Pittarn was a very long paved road. It ran right down the middle of town - from one end of the crater to the other.

Under the late afternoon sun people walked by slowly, almost leisurely.

Some even spoke.

A few cars passed by without making much of a noise. Morgan Kade felt like a sleepwalker.

- Or a fish in a tank, he said to himself without moving his lips.

That was more like it, some stupid fish in a tank.

Morgan hadn't seen a fish since he was a small child on another planet.

In just another hour the last light of day would be gone. Standing there by the side of the road, waiting for the traffic lights to change, he felt as if this day had already ended. The air he was breathing had a sour smell to it. Even the few menacing clouds above his head seemed to be as dull and gray as the town itself.

His original plan had been to take the regular bus home. But for once he had been able to leave the office early and there was absolutely no need for him to hurry.

He might as well save the 40 piastre for the bus ticket and spend it on something else.

Walking slowly down the never-ending Pittarn, his mind drifted. Without really wanting to, he recalled a conversation he had overheard back in the office. The Senator himself was talking to the new intern, Maria Santari. Morgan was sitting in the half light right outside the Senator's office, waiting for the Senator to call him in.

- So your brother will be coming tomorrow?

- Yes, Senator.

- It is perfectly all right with me if you go to Spaceport and meet him there.

- Thank you, Sir.

- What was your brother's name, again?

- Sheen, Sir. Sheen Mallory.

- That's right. He is your adopted brother, isn't he?

- Yes, Sir. But we don't see things that way. We have been together like - always.

- It's good to have family.

- Yes, Sir. It sure is.

Morgan never knew what had persuaded the Senator to accept an intern of otherworldly descent. Seen in the light of recent events it seemed to be downright foolish. Not that he would ever accuse the Senator of doing something even slightly imprudent. But nevertheless ...

He decided to pay the nearby library a visit. While he was standing there, waiting to cross the Pittarn, a police banger passed by. Morgan marveled at the sight of the powerful vehicle. He always made a mental note of the registration numbers.

This one was GOV737.

Before entering the library, he had to present his ID badge. He placed the badge on the sensor and the door opened. He gave the camera above the entrance a friendly nod. Once inside he immediately turned left, heading for the movie section. Passing the door to the Alien Studies Department he noticed that the Senator's old poster had been replaced by a brand new design.

WE NEED YOU, it said. Below the ominous words at the top of the poster, a man with a pitchfork could be seen trying to hold someone - or something - back.

The poster was simplicity itself. Nothing more needed to be said.

Morgan continued down the aisle until he reached the movie section. It took him some time to find a suitable tape. He was quite sure that he had seen them all. Having successfully completed this important task he made his way back to the news room.

*The reason Morgan had to make do with old fashioned tapes was because of the 'representations'. Shortly after Eta 3 had been colonized, there had been a major update of the IT systems. People on Eta 3 had quickly realized the potential of this new technology. The new and improved computer systems were fully capable of outperforming, overwhelming and finally taking over the senses of local inhabitants by feeding the central nervous system and the brain with a radically altered input. In a short time, there were two bank robberies and a string of grisly murders. The common denominator was the fact that innocent people had been coerced into doing things they otherwise would never have agreed to. Victims mostly experienced the effect of the new technology as a visual hallucination, but tactile input added considerably to the reality of the simulation. A full implementation of this technology was called a representation.*

*Then came the ban.*

*Obviously, it was no use scaling back the computer systems. Once the technology was known, it was sure to be replicated. It was therefore decided that all of Eta 3 from that point and onwards would only use analogue electronic systems. This had the further advantage that analogue systems and peripherals could be produced locally, while all the fancy stuff was import only.*

*Shortly after every last person on Eta 3 had to hand over all of their binary equipment to the authorities. Then they had to buy new analogue equipment - CRT TVs, tape recorders, etc.*

**Sitting in the semi darkness** of the news room, looking at the latest news, Morgan almost managed to forget about himself.

*Ritzie Mayor from Patriot News was interviewing a colonial official:*

- This is Ritzie Mayor live from Kepi 4. I am here on your behalf, talking to Colonel Shinburg.

- Colonel, exactly where were you at the time of the incident?

- Right where I was supposed to be, namely here at my desk in the Planetary High Command Building.

- When did you first notice that something was out of the ordinary?

- Unfortunately, the DMAS sensors weren't working all that well, so ...

- What is the DMAS?

- It stands for Distant Monitoring Alarm System and it is an array of sensors placed in a wide orbit around Kepi 4. These sensors are, of course, also in use on other planets throughout the Empire. The DMAS system is configured to detect incoming objects from outer space and subsequently alert High Command staff. The general idea is for us to receive a warning, a heads up so to speak, before something - or someone - hits us.

- Were those sensors malfunctioning on that particular day?

- Not all of them. Luckily, one sensor triggered an alarm and that was when I first became aware of the incoming threat.

- What was your first reaction.

- I tried to establish the precise nature of the incoming object. But the data set provided by the faulty system was very limited. I could only conclude that an unidentified object was approaching Kepi 4 - and that this something would impact in less than one hour.

- So, what did you do?

- I contacted the duty officer in command at SpaceCom and urgently requested the destruction of the incoming object.

- How did they react to such a dramatic request.

- Very professionally, indeed. They verified the data and in less than 4 minutes they launched the Freedom missile that successfully obliterated the object.

- Do we know what that object really was?

- No, unfortunately we don't. After being hit by the intercepting missile, the alien object broke into many smaller pieces. They all burned out shortly after entering the lower part of the atmosphere.

- So we will never know for sure whether this was an alien spaceship or just another large rock from outer space?

- No, but this incident certainly highlights the need for constant vigilance. Even if this was nothing more than a large stone, it could have caused serious damage. Especially if it had made its way through the atmosphere and crashed down in a densely populated area. Here on Kepi 4 we have now repaired all our sensors and thoroughly overhauled our surveillance procedures. People have a right to know that they are safe.

- We have your back.

Saying these last words, Colonel Shinburg looked straight into the camera.

Morgan Kade did not need to be told that Kepi 4 was one of the first exoplanets to be included in the Empire. He was also well aware that this was not the first time he had seen this particular interview. But it still managed to give him a good feeling. Out there, they were doing their job. Somewhere, somebody was doing their best to protect him.

The good feeling lasted right until the library door closed behind him without a sound and he was back out on the Pittarn.

**In the Town Hall of Shomonomu** Triarz Pesty was preparing for the upcoming election. From his window on the 15th floor of the Town Hall tower, Triarz could see both ends of the Pittarn. Mostly because it was a particularly clear day. The town of Shomonomu was situated in the middle of an old and strangely elongated meteor crater. Instead of blowing away, polluted air had a tendency to stay inside the confines of the old crater, where it obscured the view and made sensitive people cough and swear.

Being a senior town hall clerk, Triarz had already participated in several elections and he prided himself of having a 6th sense that told him who would be the winner. Only this time around he did not seem to have a clue. According to conventional wisdom an administration who did well with the money also had a good chance of winning the upcoming election. Judged by this standard the incumbent administration ought to be a safe bet.

9

But there was something in the air, a wind of change perhaps, new arguments being brought to the table, something ...

Shomonomu was the biggest town on the planet, but the city dwellers numbered only little more than one million. The law mandated that elections were to be analogue only, meaning that every vote had to be recorded on paper. No other method could be used.

Therefore, Triarz was a busy man. Ten voting places would each receive 100,000 ballots and one hundred ballot boxes. The remaining paraphernalia, mostly furniture and office equipment, was already in place at the ten sites.

When Triarz was younger, the municipality used to store all perishable materials in the basement of Town Hall. But on one occasion, during a failed atmospheric experiment, the lower floors of the building were inundated with water and, among many other things, all of the stored voting materials were lost. It had therefore been decided to move any such perishable items to the upper regions of the Town Hall tower.

To a complete stranger the preparations would look like a well-rehearsed ritual. Triarz Pesty would make one set of voting materials at a time. 100 packages of 1,000 ballots, each weighing exactly one Libre - every last one sealed with a blue safety ribbon and his personal stamp - and 100 ballot boxes.

When each set was finished, helping hands would carry the sealed packages and the empty ballot boxes down to a waiting truck. The truck would drive away to its final destination, duly escorted by a police banger. Like a high priest of democracy Triarz would return to his place of work on the 15th floor, preparing the next lot.

Still, election day was more than a week away.

*It sure was a great honor that he left the house in my care. I had gotten so used to him making all the important decisions that I almost dreaded being alone. At one point I tried to persuade him not to go. I told him that our kind has no tradition of traveling to other worlds. I told him that once he was there, he would be all alone. His answer was that he couldn't care less. If his protégé was going, so was he. There was nothing in this world - or the next - which could possibly keep him from sponsoring her. Then, before I knew it, they were already gone. Following their departure I had enough to do with the house and Sheen and Maria's parents and all. The hours went by like minutes and all of a sudden the letter arrived. Sheen had been admitted to the same place of higher learning that his sister had been attending these last two years. Soon we were on our way. I told myself that I had no tradition of going to other worlds. I told myself that except for Cat, I would be all alone. But in reality I felt exactly the same way as he did. Nothing could prevent me from sponsoring Sheen. Nothing. Ever.*

**Senator Burling had never** been first in line to anything. He had bowed and scraped in order to get his first job in the administration. Since then, he had had to work hard for every little promotion. Every small step forward had been earned with long hours of hard labor. Therefore, the Senator did not believe in coincidence or good luck or any such nonsense. He believed in meticulous planning and stringent execution. He believed that in the end only hard-working, dedicated men such as himself would prevail. Here and now he planned to win the upcoming election and topple the incumbent Prime Minister and his ruling party, The Democratic Advance.

Right now, for one brief minute, he was alone. The office was empty. He had given Morgan Kade the rest of the day off and the new intern was on her way to SpacePort to pick up her brother. Senator Burling hummed pleasantly while rearranging the office furniture.

When his 'guests' finally arrived, he was ready. The table was set for 6. The presentation papers were in place. Drinks and snacks, too.

Shortly after, the man from the TV station stared at page three.

*- How is this going to help us with regard to representations,* he asked.

Senator Burling sighed.

- We both know that the Representations Act will not be an easy one to repeal. I can fully understand that in your line of work you are anxious to enhance your offerings to the general public. But we must consider just why it is that this law came into being in the first place and, quite frankly, some portions of the law work to our advantage. What we are planning is to implement a reality based scheme that the electorate will find straightforward and plausible. If we use any form of digital representations, or other trickery, people will immediately cry foul. What we are hoping to gain is a de facto victory that no one in their right mind will dare to question. You need not be concerned, however, in the long run all of your needs will be provided for.

The man from the TV station seemed to be satisfied. At least he did not pursue this line of inquiry any further.

- *Will it be possible to do something about our editorial crisis,* said the lady from the big newspaper.

- Your leading board members are fully aware of your financial troubles. I have a meeting with one of them next week. There I will present him with our suggestions, including a new line of credit. We have every reason to believe that in the coming weeks you are going to sell a lot of newspapers due to the campaigning - and the other activities we are about to implement.

- *You can assure me that the editor in chief will not be a part of this solution?*

- I can guarantee that the new editorial management will be more in tune with our wishes, if that is what you want to hear.

- *Thank you, Senator.*

- My pleasure.

- *Talking about that line of credit,* said the little man from the bank. *The newspaper business will not be a problem, we can easily do that up front. But we need alternative mechanisms in order to fund some of the more nefarious activities that we cannot openly support. Perhaps we could quite simply lose some money on philanthropic adventures and covertly channel these funds to our partners?*

- I suggest that you and I discuss this later. Then you can present me with actual proposals, right?

- *Yes, Sir.*

The man at the end of the table made himself heard. It was obvious that his suit was very expensive.

- *How about corporate taxes,* he asked. *If our companies are supposed to pay for these so-called nefarious activities, we expect some kind of compensation.*

- Fair enough, Senator Burling answered. Like other incoming administrations, we expect an economic uptick following the election. When things are going obviously well, we will reduce corporate taxes by 25%.

The man in the suit seemed to be satisfied.

- *Considering surveillance*, the man from the secret police asked. *I hope the amendments to the ban on digital representations are not too far away into the future. The analogue methods we have in place right now are terribly old fashioned and quite insufficient.*

- I appreciate that you are eager to do the job at hand, but as of now the only revolution we expect is that of our own. But I promise you that as soon as we are in office, you will be provided with all the instruments you need.

Once again, the man from the secret police looked as if he was not there.

- *You are aware*, said the man from the armed forces, *that given our present budget we are not able to fight all that many aliens. With regard to incoming objects, we have one - and only one - rocket to fire. This is not common knowledge. People think that we are armed and dangerous. Even if we had all the funds we could wish for, it would still take a long time before the necessary items would arrive ...*

- The things you need are all very expensive. In order to make the public approve of such spending, we need a reason. The activities we plan will inspire stress - and perhaps even fear - into the hearts and minds of all Shomonomians. I will give you my personal guarantee that in less than a full circle, you will have everything you need.

- *I hope so,* the general said, deliberately keeping his voice down. *I certainly hope so.*

Soon after the meeting ended. Senator Burling was pleased. It had been a good and productive meeting.

*I could not get my eyes off cat. As soon as we entered the spaceport terminal building, Sheen saw Maria holding up a big sign with his name on it. Much like I had imagined, he rushed right over and threw his arms around her as if they had not seen each other for a whole lifetime. But right behind Maria I saw cat - and what a cool cat he was. Back home he had always presented himself as an ordinary black house cat, but now he was way bigger and looked more like* *a dark Cheetah. The look he gave me was frightening. It had something like **touch her and die** written all over. I wondered what had happened to him. Could this be the result of living on another planet?*

**Driving back to town** in the taxi, I was happy to sit next to Sheen. I never realized just how lonely I had been in this new world of mine. Seeing a familiar face brought out all the feelings I had worked so hard to control. Also, Sheen was so much bigger and grown-up now than he used to be. He looked just like a small adult.

- How is life in Shomonomu? Is it any fun here?

- It is a funny place, sometimes. But making new friends is not so easy. Everybody seems to know each other from childhood, school, work and so on. And they sure don't like foreigners all that much.

- I have heard about all that stuff with them being afraid of aliens. But we are not really aliens, are we?

- No, we are not. But I am just telling you now, so you won't be disappointed later. Everything is so much easier back home ...

- But you are working for this bigwig, the Senator. Isn't he the one pushing all this alien stuff to the max?

- Absolutely. It is the platform on which he is running his whole campaign. But actually he is not all that bad. See, I got the day off to come and get you.

They both laughed.

*In the airport and while we were inside the vehicle, cat never spoke a single word. I kept my quiet, too. I was already getting a feeling of how things were going.*

The speaker on the analogue TV was dressed in black.

- We are now only three days away from the election. All polls have the Democratic Advance solidly in the lead by 7 points, but *Fathers of Freedom* have made solid advances with their unrelenting demand for more protection of our civil society, which they claim is at risk. Later tonight, the spokesperson for the Fathers, the well-known and well-liked Senator Burling, will make his final pitch here on Channel 101.

**Morgan Kade knew** he had to hurry. He was still sitting in the news room. If he wanted to hear the Senator's speech - and he most certainly did - he would have to hurry home. As soon as the library door closed behind him, he saw the bus. He started running.

Later, in the apartment, the only light was the television. While he was waiting for the Senator to appear, Morgan thought of how much better television used to be. They used to have holographic communication with incredible 3D effects. But due to the ban on representations this was now a thing of the past. Morgan knew for a fact that it was also possible to manipulate a low-definition analogue picture, but that did not seem to matter much to anyone. Like everybody else, he had had to hand over his fancy holo-display and pay through the nose for this miserable replacement.

Still, a low-res TV set was way better than no TV at all.

*- Dear friends,* **the Senator said.** If there are some among you who think that I have somehow lost it - that I am resorting to fake news and big lies - it is totally understandable and I will certainly not be the one to blame you.

The election is only days away. The Democratic Advance has done a good job and should be praised. They have seen to it that our society works almost flawlessly, that the economy is stable and we are able to live acceptable - even fairly good - lives.

But, unfortunately, times have changed in unprecedented ways. Intruders from the great unknown are creeping in on us. Every day these dangers are coming closer. I am in fact quite happy to tell you that standing here in front of you on this very day I do not have a smoking gun or any incriminating evidence that I can present to you. No factual evidence at all.

But come that fateful day when I have such evidence in my possession, it may already be too late.

By now we have seen countless incidents where things from the outside wants in. On allied planets, mysterious objects have crashed through the atmosphere. We have even heard rumors about shape shifting alien agents. It is my duty to tell you that incidents of this nature are bound to happen time and time again.

My greatest fear is that *they* (his right hand made an upward gesture) are already here, only we don't recognize them, we don't see them for what they really are.

**Morgan Kade sighed with relief.** The words of the Senator were like music to his tired ears. The Senator had his back, no doubt about it.

# We Are The Aliens

Next morning there was a serious disturbance at a bus stop near the Pittarn. As a first sign of trouble, the bus never came. Soon a large number of people could be seen standing there, waiting. As time passed by the crowd got louder, bigger, and angrier. When the bus finally appeared there was a huge blast. Because of the name of a near-by theatre, it was later referred to as *the Odeon Explosion*.

A total of 16 people died and 34 were wounded. The bus itself was badly damaged and the driver was in a coma.

In the evening Senator Burling reappeared on prime-time television. He gave another riveting speech the subjects of which included aliens in outer space, aliens already on the planet, accomplices to aliens and – last, but not least – the softness with which the incumbent administration had dealt with this rather explosive subject.

- I have to speak, the Senator roared, on behalf of the bereaved families, on behalf of the public servant who is now in a coma. I have to speak for those who have lost arms and legs in this horrible incident which in my book is beyond the pale. I have to speak up now so that we can all join hands and together agree on measures needed to prevent such things from ever happening again.

While he was talking, a great majority of the good people on Eta 3 were sitting in front of their television sets, following his every word.

Outside, strange things could be seen in the skies. Streaks of blue lights moved across the heavens. Sounds could be heard in the distance. Lights flashed, as if someone was sending signals to parties unknown.

These things were, of course, reported in the news following the Senator's big speech.

**I was sitting next to Cat** outside the house where Maria lived. We both watched the low flying satellite which painted a visible blue streak across the evening skies, before it finally fell down and crashed in a remote desert on the other side of the planet.

- So much for the aliens, Cat said. These people have a lousy military. They can't even produce proper fireworks.

- The people of this world will never know, I said. They don't even know that it is only a satellite. They think it is something dangerous from out there ...

- He wants power, that is what he wants – that damned Senator.

- Yes, and the only aliens around these parts are you and me and the kids.

Cat turned his head and looked down on me.

- A pity that we can't tell them, he said.

- We need to find a soft spot in his evil plans, I said. Something we can hold on to and attack.

It so happened that the first soft spot turned out to be the bankster. He happily bankrolled each and every legal and illegal activity the Senator came up with. Then he took the rest of the money and transferred it to a secret account of his own. Cat and I made this information available to the man from the secret police.

Next morning, when the bankster's dead body was found hanging from under a bridge, the newspaper he had paid for *and* the TV station he had so generously funded both implied in their reporting that this was the work of clandestine alien supporters.

It was not enough. Cat was on my case.

- We have to do something before he gets a chance to frame the children. He wants to parade Maria and Sheen on TV as horrible alien agents. When their faces have appeared on every television set in town, you and I will have a hard time getting them out of here. We need something and we need it now.

*I couldn't help myself. I barked. Just one time.*

- I think I've got it, I told him. Just wait and see ...

**An overlooked routine** in the work of Triarz Pesty was what I had found. This discovery also made me realize that the Senator was far more meticulous than most other people. If one of his little schemes failed, he would always have a plan B to fall back on.

So rather suddenly, on the very last day before the election, Mr. Pesty – as if out of nowhere – came to the conclusion that it was his duty to inspect a voting place. It was several years since he had done any such thing. With a new-found conviction that even he himself found strange, he called the local police and demanded that a Banger with a uniformed escort should take him to a specific venue.

Upon his arrival, he started an impromptu inspection. The local staff did not disagree in any way. They all knew who he was. The Banger and the uniforms also made quite an impression.

The facility had everything Triarz needed to finish the job. At first glance he thought that everything looked fine (and way down inside he started feeling a little bit silly). But then he happened to weigh one of the one hundred packages containing the ballots.

It was a complete shock. It weighed 1.05 Libre. Not 1.0 Libre as it was supposed to, but 1.05 exactly.

And it got worse.

They all weighed 1.05 Libre.

At first poor Triarz thought that the weight itself could be the problem. Luckily there was another weight available.

The new weight faithfully reported that the packages still weighed exactly 1.05 Libre each.

This made Triarz Pesty do something that he had never done before. He took a good look at his own stamp – which most certainly looked the way it should – and then he broke the blue safety ribbon and opened the package

The package had obviously been opened and then re-sealed. Some ballots had been removed. In the middle of the stack, one hundred new ballots had been inserted. These one hundred fake ballots were all votes in favor of the Fathers of Freedom.

Triarz sat down on a chair, thoughts were racing through his head.

Then he got up and asked one of the uniforms if he could please use his safe Intercom. He called his old class mate from high school who now worked in the Ministry of Justice.

# The Reign of The Old King

Some days I will never forget. Some memories are so painful that your only wish is to get rid of them and just forget about the whole thing. But even as the never-ending years slowly turn into centuries, some days still come back to haunt me.

In one of these dreadful moments I see myself standing on the top floor of the white tower. I look out of the big panorama window, silently watching the last of our big birds flying away.

Standing there, I try in vain to remind myself of how everything that has a beginning also needs to have an end. But even now, after so many years, it does not make me feel any better.

I knew that once again time had caught up with us. An era was about to end.

The last dragon was leaving for good.

Every time I am reminded of that day, it all comes rushing back to me. I am forever standing there by the window, desperately wishing to turn back time.

Already miles away, the dragon roared its final goodbye. Much like elephants, dragons tend to seek out a quiet spot - their final resting place, so to speak. Feeling their time had come, they would go there to die. We could easily have tracked them, if only to find out where they went. But for some reason we never did.

Like abandoned husbands, we did not want to know.

- Where is that last female you promised me, I asked.

Even though I tried to keep it down, I was bitter. There was no point in hiding it. He already knew.

- Not everything works out according to schedule, he answered. It appears that my plan wasn't perfect.

His voice was eerily calm. It made me think of thin ice slowly melting on a cool spring morning.

My own feelings of being trapped alone inside of an empty, endless desert was perfectly justified by the glorious view from the highest point of the white tower. All around the Citadel there was nothing but desert and low mountains. Nothing but sand dunes and big rocks as far as the eye could see.

Finally, the big wings disappeared into the setting sun.

Our dragon days were over.

Surely, I had known for a long time that this day would come. But the reality of it was more painful than I had ever imagined. Now I realized just how much I had come to rely on these ferocious beasts.

Inside of me - and out in the real world too, where the dragons used to be - there was nothing but emptiness. For centuries the dragons had served me well. They had been my surrogate family. We had eaten the same cows, talked till late in the morning and often fought shoulder by shoulder. Now I was left with nothing but the memories.

Obviously, Terach did not experience any of the withdrawal symptoms that haunted me so badly. I knew for a fact that he had grown tired of the dragons a long time ago. He had only kept them around for my sake.

And now that it was all over, it was easy for me to see that the dragons and I were one and the same; we did not have a natural place in this world.

The dragons were the product of an alien mind, an artificial life form conceived by a genius from another planet. They never had any natural birth right; they did not belong in this world.

In the same way I was a being, somehow resembling a man, who should have died a long time ago.

But those fiery creatures and I had lived side by side in the Citadel for almost one thousand years

In this uncaring and hostile world the dragons had been my only family.

Perhaps I should have been less emotional about it. Without a doubt I should have considered more carefully just why it was that my other half did not see things the way I did. But he never talked about it.

I had a nagging feeling that the only good thing the dragons had ever done for him was to relieve him of his main burden - and that would be me. As long as the dragons were there, he never had to worry about me and my fragile state of mind.

As time went by I had come to think of him as being next to unbreakable.

A rock to lean on? *Oh, yes.*

But a shoulder to cry on? *Definitely not.*

Before long, memories of the dragons began to fade. Soon they had turned into old wives' tales. As time passed by it was obvious that ordinary people no longer believed in their existence. They were referred to in mythical terms only. Tall tales about imaginary creatures that never really existed.

And in this new reality there was absolutely nothing left for me to do. Everything was in impeccable order and we had no enemies to defeat. Our desert world was stable and everything happened just like it should.

As far as I know, we only had one problem – that would be me – and I was a wreck.

It felt like I had been cursed by life itself. Every time I tried to pull myself together and leave the white tower, the people of the Citadel would instantly recognize me and a noisy, cheering crowd would gather. Some would cry, some would scream and some would beg. The commotion was unbearable. The end result was always the same. I would soon find myself back home in the white tower, very frustrated and all alone.

An evil twist of fate had turned our beloved tower into a prison.

**Seeing the last dragon fly away** made me both happy *and* sad. For a long time now, the dragons had been a pain, a constant reminder of my father's type 1 population and their sudden demise. Bringing these creatures back to life in the shape of dragons turned out to be a major mistake. Most of the time it felt like I was mocking the dead.

Obviously, I had repeated my father's mistake in a bad way.

It was disturbing, to say the least.

Just imagine that you hear a familiar voice behind you. You turn around to greet your old friend, but instead of the person you used to know you find a horrible monster, bigger and more sinister than a mad elephant bull - and even though you have absolutely no need for such a beast, all of a sudden you have no less than five of them.

The dragons were a nuisance through and through.

But Haran loved the dragons and they loved him.

So from my point of view, the whole thing was a fiasco. Except for Haran and the money. No one dared to challenge the Dragon King. The neighbors were so afraid of the dragons that they always paid the tributes long before they were due. That was a good thing, but before long we had so much gold stashed away that I ran out of storage rooms and had to build new vaults under the laboratory.

The caravans also paid a lot of taxes. There was a constant influx of travelers who spent good money in the Citadel. We were rich like no one before us had ever been.

In the end I left all the dragon business to Haran. He did all the feeding and the herding and the flying. Having nothing to do with all this tedious business, I was free to do as I pleased. Those were the terms of our dragon deal.

But when the last dragon finally flew away, Haran was left with nothing. I had seen this coming, but I did not know what to do about it.

It was like a nightmare come true.

All day long Haran would just sit inside the white tower, sulking.

I had to do something about it, so one day I said to him: Why don't you go out and have some fun?

We happened to be standing in front of a big mirror. He looked straight into the mirror and told me that there was no fun to be had. Whenever he stepped out of the front door, he would be surrounded by agitated citizens who cheered and screamed and tried to hold on to him, while others would beg and plead and cry.

- I am too well known for any such thing. If only I could go to the nearest tavern and have something to drink, and maybe a good fight or two - that would be something. But they all know me. The king cannot sit down and drink with his subjects.

- Then we shall deceive them. We will change your appearance radically and they will never know who you are.

- We have done that already. How long will it take this time, a couple of years? A decade - or maybe more?

- No, nothing like that. Last time we did it very slowly so that people would not notice.

- Since then I have improved the procedure quite a lot. What I am talking about can be done in a matter of seconds.

So we did it. We made a new man.

We tried to keep a number of bodily features approximately the same size. Our new friend would be of the same height as the old king. Certain, very personal parts would also be of the same proportions. But the new man was slimmer and more agile - and quite handsome. When we had the dimensions of the body right, we spent a long time working on the face. Certainly, when it comes to human beauty, I am not the best of judges. But in the end a new person appeared in the mirror, and a real charmer he was. Our new man had perfect teeth and a flashing smile. Even the hair was perfect.

What should we call him?

Haran did not hesitate:

- How about Ben.

Ben was a ray of light; from the very start he brightened up our world. Right inside our front door there was a small room. In this room we installed a couple of oil lamps, a mirror and two sets of clothing; one set for Ben and one set for the old king.

When that was in place, I summoned the Captain of the Guards. He was a tall, gaunt desert man. Everything about him was dark. His hair was dark, his skin was dark and his eyes were even darker. He went by the name of Shrall. His haggard face never revealed any emotions. It was said that no man inside the Citadel walls had ever seen a smile on his face.

Now he was standing right inside the front door, respectfully holding his helmet under his left arm.

- A distant cousin of mine will be visiting, I said. He will be staying with us for a while. His name is Ben. I am told that he is very fond of drinking and gambling and fooling around with women. You are supposed to assist him and help him out of any trouble he might get himself into - without making too much of a fuss about it. Your job is to limit any damage he might do and to protect him from suffering bodily harm. I am talking about bodyguards out of uniform and adequate instructions to the regular guards on duty. If everything works out as planned, you will meet him here tomorrow night at ten o'clock outside the door.

Shrall bowed. He did not say a single word, but the matter was settled.

**The following evening,** I found myself sitting comfortably at a table in a big tavern called The Hairy Dragon. Sitting next to me were two bodyguards, courtesy of Shrall. They had obviously been told that I was somehow related to the Old King himself, so they were *very* respectful. I smiled reassuringly and ordered beer. Soon they were both more than half drunk, telling me all about their families and the happy things they hoped their future would bring.

Soon other people joined our little party and we kept the waiter busy. When The Hairy Dragon finally closed for the night I found myself surrounded by a cheerful band of inebriated fools. We were a jolly company, laughing and singing, passing quiet streets, and walking down back roads - trying to find another place where the lights were still on.

I was quite pleased. Being treated like a normal person was exactly what I had been longing for. I pretended to be drunk, but I wasn't. I was just having a good time and getting the most out of it.

As it turned out there was only one place left to go. It was called The Oasis. Inside, the ceiling was low and the lights were dim. The waiter greeted us and led us down to one of only two vacant tables. One of my bodyguards immediately sat down in a corner and fell asleep. The other one was still around, but he looked a bit pale.

- It's a good thing that I don't really need them, I thought to myself. If anything happened, I would certainly be the one to protect them and not the other way around.

It did not matter. This was my town.

One of my 'fools' started telling a story about a girl he once knew. In order to avoid her husband, he always went to see her before noon. But one day the husband unexpectedly returned from work and my new friend had to jump out through the window. He showed me a scar on his right leg to prove that it was indeed a true story. Even though I laughed politely, the story was more than a little boring.

I ordered more drinks and saluted my last bodyguard. He was embarrassed by the fact that his mate had dozed off. He looked at his sleeping comrade. Then he looked back at me and made a gesture saying 'I am sorry'.

I shook my head and indicated that it was of no consequence.

New customers sat down at the last free table. I saw two big men and a woman. They looked like travelers fresh in from the desert. But that couldn't be. It was late night and the gates had been closed for hours.

When their outerwear came off, it was obvious that the men were master and slave. The slave was a huge black man in his prime. His master was a seasoned mercenary, no doubt about it. Seeing right through his clothes, I immediately spotted the small, but razor sharp javelin he was hiding. And then I saw the woman.

# Some People Have All the Luck

I am the youngest child of a troubled family. My big brother is the oldest. He is the only product of my father's first marriage.

Father never talks about his first marriage. I believe his first wife is dead, but I don't know how or when.

My mother also brought a child into the marriage, my older sister. My brother and my sister never got along. They were always fighting. But they both seemed to like me. Life is strange that way.

We never had enough money. Father used to work as a hired hand for the local farmers. Mother went to the marketplace every morning, hoping that someone would hire her to do something, no matter what. We never seemed to make it, but at least we were not starving *every* day.

My big brother is not very smart and he always had trouble with lots of things. If he was not fighting with my sister, he would be fighting with someone else instead. It never did him any good. Father used to beat him up on a regular basis - and then my brother would go out and beat up somebody else, just to get even.

I guess that is pretty much how things work out.

The years of my childhood passed by and with every passing year my sister looked better and better. Even though he did not really like her, my brother soon had to fight a lot of boys just to keep them away from her. The way father looked at her made all of us uncomfortable. She wasn't his child. That was a little something we were all aware of.

She never called him dad, she used his first name instead.

One day when she was 14 years old she came home in tears. Her clothes were torn and she had bruises on her arms and legs. For once we were all alone.

- You cannot tell anybody about this.

She grabbed me by the arms and shook me violently.

- If your father understands what has happened to me, he will not let me be ...

I knew that it was true. So I nodded.

She fixed herself up and the rest of the day she pretended that nothing had happened.

But somehow things had changed.

A couple of weeks later, a band of mercenaries drifted into town.

The owner of the inn was the only one who liked them. But that was because they stayed at his inn and he made a lot of money.

Then one day my sister did not come home.

Mother made a fuss about it, so at long last father got up and went looking for her. I followed him at a distance.

At the inn there were lots of people and music could be heard. Father went in. That did not come as a surprise. I quickly placed myself next to one of the windows, gazing at the scenery inside.

And there I saw my sister. She was doing some sort of a belly dance, standing on a table in the back of the room. A rowdy crowd inside was cheering her on.

She looked fantastic. Her hair flowed around her head and shoulders as red hot fire. She wore an outfit, the like of which I had never seen before.

My father stood at the back of the crowd, who were clapping and cheering her on. Obviously, he did not know how to handle the situation.

When the music stopped, he passed through the men, went up to the table and tried to drag her down.

A big fellow quickly got himself between father and my sister. My window was slightly open and I only stood a few steps away from them. I could hear every word they said.

- What are you up to?

The big man looked at my father with a frown on his face.

- This is my daughter. I've come to get her.

- No, he is not, my sister called out from upon the table. He only wants me for himself.

- Now is that so, the big man said. He looked father straight in the eyes.

- Maybe you'd better get going.

Father tried to make a move on the man. But it was hopeless. The big man easily fended off father's clumsy attack. Then from out of nowhere he produced a short, curved sword. With the sword right under his nose, father stopped dead in his tracks. He did not move so much as a finger.

That was the end of it.

**My sister came** home to see me and mother while father was working. My older brother was out working too.

- *Please come home. These men are not good for you. In the end you will be unhappy. People will think of you as a whore,* mother said to her.

- *You are probably right,* my sister answered. *But what is the alternative. Must I really stay here and marry some stupid farmer? No, mother. I am going away.*

She patted me on the head, as if I was a dog, and then she was already gone.

# The Siege

After we arrived safe and sound back home on P336 there was no reason for Likander to stay. He and his fellow pilot left for home. We actually had two full days of peace. Then the Marauders returned.

It seems that in the real world things never change. Everything happened just like before. Only this time we - the forces on the ground - were a little better prepared than last time.

So was the enemy.

Every time they saw something moving on the ground below they bombed it viciously. They also bombed both of our domes, but soon enough they concentrated all of their energy on the smaller one. Just like before they used solar energy to direct a constant beam of destructive energy down on the old dome.

I had more than one conversation with Control. In the beginning he was rather upbeat, but as time went by and the unrelenting bombardment from above continued, he seemed to be more and more concerned.

- It is a shame that we don't have a better guidance system.

- What do we need a guidance system for, I asked.

- We need a mechanism to better focus our energy beams. As it is now, I can target anything inside the atmosphere. But it is not possible to target the enemy in outer space.

- It is a shame that Likander had to go home, I said. Maybe he could have constructed the thing you are talking about.

- Yes, he would have been perfect. But the way it is now, I have nothing to work with. The original flight computer on which I am based was designed for a commercial transporter, not for a battle cruiser. So apart from the amendments your own father and NeLo made, there is nothing I can use against the enemy.

- Then we must continue and do our very best, hoping that in the end the enemy will give up and go away.

- Actually, there is one option, one more thing we can try. As far as I understand, you brought home a prisoner and Likander left him here, in your care so to speak.

I must have looked worried, because Control suddenly changed his approach.

- We have already talked about *your* father. You must have realized that in a certain way the person I am talking about is actually *my* father. With regard to weaponry and programming he is totally on par with Likander. Can we really afford to ignore this opportunity?

- But can we really afford to set him free? If he gets out of the pod, he will take this planet by whatever means he has at his disposal. I am no match for him, I know that already.

- True, but I have a suggestion ...

**Jean and Juliana were** looking for Sil.

The twins stopped in front of Mozil.

- Mozil, they said. Have you seen Sil?

- No. I believe she is with Azil.

- Well, she should be. But we just found out that she is not and (the twins said exactly the same things out loud at exactly the same time) because she is so tiny we cannot help but worry.

- It's all right. Sil is not as fragile as she looks.

- Are you sure about that?

- Yes, absolutely. Or at least, so says Azil.

- We should go find Patil, Jean said to Juliana. He will know where we can find her. Juliana nodded.

- Bye, Mozil. The girls smiled their sweetest smile and off they went.

They found Patil in the Registry Room. Like always, he was working. Staring intensely at the monitor in front of him, his fingers moved effortlessly across the keyboard.

Again the girls spoke with a voice that was one and the same.

- Patil, have you seen Sil? We have been looking all over, but we can't seem to find her.

- She is in the garden, he answered without looking up. She is at her favorite spot. The one with the big tree.

- Thank you, Patil.

Patil did not even raise his head. He never looked at Jean and Juliana, who had already left the room.

They found Sil sitting in the shade of her favorite tree. She looked like a fairy. Everybody that saw her, immediately felt that she was the cutest thing on the whole planet.

- What are you doing, said Jean. We have been looking for you everywhere.

- We even went to ask your brother, Juliana continued while her twin sister was spinning round like a top. How come he always knows where you are.

- I am looking for the entrance, Sil answered. I know there is an entrance here. If I sit really still and concentrate, then maybe I can find it.

- An entrance to ... what?

- I don't know, silly Jean. How could I know when I haven't found it yet.

The twins stopped talking. For a little while they were all silent.

# High Up in The Emptiness

It started out as just another morning, high above Draco.

Honestly, I don't know why we have two names for the same planet. The official name is Draco. But we always call it Lonesome Planet, obviously because it is the only planet orbiting its star. It is the most tantalizing object I have ever encountered. No matter where I have been or what I have done – ever since the first time I saw that damned planet, I have thought about it each and every day. This planetary infatuation of mine has caused me to lose everything I ever had.

When you are in space, words such as morning, evening and night lose their meaning. The starlight will always find you and the night will never come.

But on that fateful day it was 'morning' in the sense that I had been sleeping. Together with a lot of other crew members I was getting up and preparing for our next shift.

In the control room I had added one personal item, my first invention. A solid-state neutrino detector. With this device I had established my reputation as a scientist. Out of sheer vanity I brought it with me wherever I went. So here it was, firmly bolted on to a wall in the control room of the spaceship I commanded.

I barely had the time to sit down in the Captain's chair before a crew member gently tapped me on the shoulder and pointed to this particular device. It was indeed counting neutrinos. It was counting much more neutrinos than it should. I hurriedly established the direction from where the neutrinos were coming. Looking back, I do remember that I was suddenly shivering all over. Doing my best not to scream, I enlarged this area on the big control room monitor. The entire room had turned dead silent. Everybody looked at what I was doing. I also put the neutrino counter on-screen. The numbers were running wild.

Then there was a new star. As a flower out of nowhere the Supernova appeared right before our eyes. We all felt doom and despair hitting us like a million hammers. I remained standing up. Some crew members were on their knees. Others just stood there, petrified. We all knew what had happened. Our star had exploded. Our home world was no more.

In hindsight it is easy to say that all of this already happened 4 years ago. That the terrible light we saw at that particular moment in space and time was just a reminder of the actual horror. But I tell you that the desperation, the ice cold feeling of being left behind, the indisputable loss of our home world, the loss of everything - these feelings were unbearably real.

While the light from the supernova grew stronger and covered more and more of the big screen, I had to sit down in the Captain's chair. I could not stand that light. I had to close my eyes and turn my face away from it. I could not even look at it.

Deep inside of me, in the only part of my mind that was still functioning, I came to the conclusion that we no longer had any business at Lonesome Planet. In that moment my only wish was to get as far away from that light as possible.

So, I cursed and screamed like a demon and made the men work harder than ever before. I kicked and yelled and cried until we were ready to depart and then, as our spaceships slowly moved away, I just stood there, looking back at Draco.

The planet that swallowed all of my hopes and dreams before it finally kicked me out.

# Growing Pains

When I met Fierter, I really believed that I had struck pure gold. Back then my life was miserable. All day long I had to be very careful and never get caught. If I got caught, I would be raped - again. And if my stepfather found out that I was not a virgin any more, then ...

So, I was careful. Always very, very careful.

Then one day I met Fierter outside the inn. I must have looked scared, because he immediately tried to calm me down. He promised that he wouldn't hurt me and invited me in.

It turned out that he already had company. He had a big black slave named Gondar. To me it looked like Gondar could handle just about everything the world could throw at him, but to my surprise he obediently did every little thing Fierter told him to do.

The other mercenaries also seemed to have a high opinion of Fierter.

I was having a good time. It was the first time I had seen the inn from the inside. Of course, I got a little drunk. But not too much.

That night I did not go home. I stayed with Fierter in his room at the inn. It was way better than being raped in some alley.

Next morning, we toured the market. Luckily my mother wasn't there.

Fierter bought me some new clothes.

When we got home, he asked me to put on the outfit and then he tried to teach me how to belly dance.

Three days later we left town for good.

The first couple of weeks were really nice. I was in love with Fierter and I firmly believed that he was also in love with me. That was how naive I was.

One evening in the next town, Fierter was playing some kind of game. I did not pay much attention to it. But in the end, he lost quite a lot of money.

So, he came to me.

*After the first couple of men, I had no more feelings for Fierter. But he was a good pimp. That is how I remember him, Fierter the good pimp.*

In Farshi we had trouble with the local goons and Fierter killed two of their foot soldiers. After that he was in a great hurry to get as far away from Farshi as he possibly could.

So we joined a caravan and did our best not to stand out in any way. For days we marched down an endless caravan road that tossed and turned among the sand dunes.

The heat almost killed me.

In the dead of night, we arrived at the white Citadel. The moon was out and the fabled desert town looked very appealing. We should, of course, have waited patiently outside the city walls until morning came and the gates would open. But Fierter wanted in.

He cried out to a couple of guards on the city wall high above us. After a lot of haggling, they agreed on a price and sent down a rope ladder. On my way up, I was scared and tried not to look down. Looking up I could see the full moon. It felt as if I was crawling up the ladder and straight into it.

I knew that Fierter was desperately low on funds. He must have given the guards almost everything we had. That could only mean one thing – even if it was very late, tonight we had to make some money, one way or the other.

As we walked down peaceful, moonlit streets I felt a shiver running down my spine. To me, our arrival at this wonderful place was like magic. But I could clearly see that Fierter did not feel anything special about it at all. He just kept on walking, like any good mercenary should, Gondar right behind him.

We soon arrived at the only late night joint – The Oasis, so said the sign above the door. I could not read the letters, but there was a little painting of a blue lake and a few palms.

The waiter escorted us to the only vacant table in the back of the establishment.

We were not alone. At another table a motley crew had gathered. I remember thinking that they must have been at it for a while, because one of them, a young man, sat sleeping with his back to the wall. There was a couple of old-timers, another young man and a big fellow. Before long the big bloke ordered drinks. He paid for all of it, too.

Looking at Fierter, I knew exactly what he was planning to do.

It did not take long before I was sitting at that other table, right next to the big guy. I noticed two things. He was sitting with his back against the wall and he was most certainly taking an interest in me.

I smiled, invitingly.

Very slowly Gondar moved into position.

At a certain point Fierter seemed to be ready for the grande finale.

He got up and walked over to where I was sitting. Gondar gave the young fellow next to the big guy a good push that landed him on the floor, almost next to his sleeping comrade.

Fierter put both hands on the table, smiled his most devilish smile and said: *My good man, what do you think you are doing with my woman* ...

And that was as far as he got.

During the relatively short time I had been with Fierter, we had already used this particular routine several time. We had even practiced it. I knew the continuation very well. Fierter would take out his sword and threaten the mark to give him all of his money, or else ...

Only, this time it did not work.

The big fellow got up and with a powerful kick he turned the table over. Fierter had to jump backwards. Then, as if out of nowhere, the stranger suddenly had a big, shiny sword.

Valiantly, Fierter still tried to do his best.

He managed to stay on his feet.

He tried to get his own sword out.

But he didn't quite make it.

There was a flash of light and a loud swoosh and Fierter's head was rolling on the floor.

I am not sure, but I think I heard myself screaming.

Almost immediately soldiers came into the room. They all wore the same black uniform as the ones who guarded the town walls. Poor Gondar was standing still with both arms in the air, looking at several drawn swords all pointing straight at him.

- Are you hurt, their leader asked the big man.

He just shook his head.

The officer went over to the wall where one young man was sitting down, looking bewildered, and the other young man was still fast asleep. He gave the sleeper a good kick - but he did not wake up, he just fell over.

- I am sorry, Sir. They were no good.

- No need to be sorry, the big man replied. I like them. They will accompany me again tomorrow.

The officer looked at him in disbelief.

- As you wish, was all he said.

Although I was very frightened, I understood a few things.

The leader of the soldiers treated the big fellow with the utmost respect. So he had to be someone important.

And I was in serious trouble. No doubt about it. These people would not hear any excuses. We had tried to make a move on a very important member of their society and it utterly failed.

Fierter was dead, his severed head still lying on the floor. The look on Gondar's face told me that he expected to die any minute. And I was just a silly girl ...

- Please come with me.

A big hand landed on my shoulder.

I did the only thing I could do. I turned around and followed him into the night.

In my naivety I thought I had it all figured out. But when we arrived at his home, the sheer size of it left me speechless.

The night was almost over and morning light was slowly seeping in. Before my tired eyes I saw a building three or four times the size of the inn back home.

We had walked the short distance from The Oasis to his home without an escort of any kind. But as soon as we approached the house, a manservant opened the front door. Inside, a maid was busy lighting torches and lamps.

I had never seen a dwelling the like of this man's. He had fine furniture, paintings on the walls, carpets on the floor.

The more I saw, the worse I felt inside. I still believed that I was about to be subjected to some gruesome punishment. Maybe he was just toying around with me; a little pleasure before the final act.

I looked at him and shivered even more.

Even in this state of constant fright I noticed a few things.

He did not wear any armor, no bodily protection at all.

And also the big shiny sword that had so effortlessly severed poor Fierter's head from his body was nowhere to be seen.

Well, he must have left it somewhere ...

The manservant came over and very discretely gestured that I should follow him.

We went to the back of the house and he led me to the bath room.

The tub was already filled. The manservant left me at the door, but soon a maid appeared. She was really nice to me. With a smiling face she showed me the various kinds of soap, the towels and the perfume. Later, when I lay in the bathtub it was like heaven. The maid also took my clothes and laid out some new ones.

Afterwards I looked into the mirror.

I don't mean to boast, but what I saw in the mirror that morning was the best version of me, ever.

When I came back into his quarters, the big man looked me over.

- Ho ho, he said. You look like a goddamn princess.

I guess I don't have to tell you how that morning ended ...

# Find of A Lifetime

One 'morning' not long after our departure from Draco, I woke up in my cabin. The turmoil inside of me and the monotony of traveling through space had made me lose any sense of time. I relied on our military calendar and followed it rigorously. Following a well-defined scheme like that actually made me feel a little better.

I had hardly closed the door behind me, before an ensign came to me with a message. The officer in charge informed me that we were rapidly approaching a small manufactured object. We were not going full speed, but even at our present velocity we would soon overtake it.

I hurried to the control room and inspected the data. The object was made of metal. From the shape alone it was clear to see that this was not a natural object.

Curiosity got the better of me.

We slowed down and pulled it in with a tractor beam. In the rear end of the ship we had a reinforced compartment, designed for unstable ammunition and well suited for this purpose. Soon enough the object was lying on the floor. I went in there, followed by two technicians. I gave a voice command to shut the heavy door behind us and then I waited patiently until it had closed completely.

The object seemed to be some kind of rocket. It had a small engine at the back, but it was obvious that this alone could not provide enough propulsion for a planetary launch.

What could it be? Perhaps some sort of transportation, launched from a another spaceship ...

The thing was lying inert on the floor. It was about three times my own length. In the weak artificial gravity field our ship could provide it did not weigh much. If we had been down on a planet, it would have weighed quite a lot.

I probed it with a scanner. There was active circuitry in the front parts – and more at the back, near the diminutive engine.

I slowly scanned it again, working my way back to the front. Halfway there, I found something interesting; two adjacent areas with a certain amount of magnetism just under the metal surface. I decided that this was probably the lock. So how about the key?

The first thing that came to my mind was to connect the two magnetic areas with a weak current. Doing so, the middle part of the rocket-like thing came apart. Two sliding doors slowly retracted. What appeared before our eyes was quite unexpected. Behind a screen of transparent material, lying on a velvet cushion-like material, was a woman.

Don't ask me why I immediately came to the conclusion that the alien was a female. Surely, she did not look like any woman I had ever seen before. She had two legs and two arms. But these features were strangely elongated and her face was – confusing.

There could be no doubt that what we had found was some kind of lifeboat. The whole thing had undoubtedly been released from a larger vessel. The woman inside had then drifted slowly across the universe, hibernating inside her alien pod.

But was she still alive?

At this point my scientific training kicked in. I checked the location of our first encounter and the course of her lifeboat. The facts were there, but they did not convey any meaning.

Then I tried to hack the circuitry inside the lifeboat. It was a rather disappointing experience. Whoever had made it, knew very well what they were doing.

And there were no markings, no identification. Nothing.

I discussed these facts with the technicians. I asked for their opinion of how to proceed. The prudent thing would be to close the lifeboat doors, seal off the compartment we were in and wait for a more stable situation.

But again, curiosity got the better of us.

**When I woke up**, I soon realized that I had failed to reach my destination. The pod had been opened and three strange creatures were looking down on me. Believe me - when I say strange, I mean *really* strange.

It was obvious that I was inside a spaceship, so these people must have found me. Luckily the air seemed to be breathable. The aliens carefully helped me to sit up. My head was reeling from the long hibernation.

I managed to open the compartment behind the cushion. The liquid was still there and so was the emergency medication. Soon I was feeling much better. Meanwhile, my new shipmates waited patiently.

Chances were that we did not speak the same language (so far not a single word has been spoken).

I inserted the universal translator into my left ear. One of my saviors wore a markedly different outfit, so I guessed that maybe he was in command. I addressed him:

- Thank you for taking me in, I said. Can you tell me where I am?

He seemed to be a bit flustered about the fact that he could understand what I just said. I tapped the translator with one hand while pointing to my lips with the other.

He seemed to understand.

- When you are ready, we can go to our control room and I can give you our coordinates. But basically, we are out in the middle of nowhere.

- And what may you be doing here – out in the middle of nowhere?

- That is a long story, I am afraid ...

Later, in his control room, on the big monitor I could see the rest of his small fleet. Only then did I realize who had taken me in. I knew the shape of these spaceships only too well.

I was in the hands of the enemy. These were marauder ships.

# Lost in The Fog

**I often sit here** looking at myself in the mirror. It is not even my own mirror. But I take it for granted that the face in the mirror is actually mine. I wish it wasn't. But really, it has to be. Right now I've got to get up and get dressed. I have to walk all the way over to Liesl and beg her for some dope. I really have to do a lot of begging these days, haven't I?

Well, good old Liesl. What would I do without her? Wonder if I can still find my way to that trailer of hers? What the fuck would I do if I ever got lost for real and couldn't even find my way back here.

I could call Harry. Good old Harry. But then I have to give him some of the dope. If I get any dope at all, that is. Maybe she'll just throw me flat out on my face. Maybe she ought to.

I am worthless.

I don't know why I always have to feel this way. The way things are, I don't know very much at all. I just sit here and glare at my own stupid face in the mirror. When there is no more dope, I have to get out of here and do some more begging.

If it wasn't for Liesl, I'd probably be doing tricks down at the gas station. They say those truckers pay well. It's probably another big lie, but maybe …

Fuck, I really have to go see Liesl. Get your ass moving, girl.

What was my name again? These days my reality is like something shrouded in a mist. Anyway, they all call me a bitch or a skank. *Get out of my store, bitch. What are you bitching about, you fucking skank.* Those are the kind of responses I get all the time.

And here comes Harry.

I'm impressed. He made it here all by himself.

He looks as if he got swallowed by a big whale and then it somehow spit him right out again. But never mind that. Harry is OK – as long as he doesn't run away with my dope. That is the one thing I just can't tolerate.

One of these days I should buy myself a gun. A big fancy gun.

Then I could just walk up to all of them and say – *Hey you. You all called me bitch, didn't you? Are you going to say that straight to my face again?* And I will just wave that big shiny gun under their noses, real slow. That would do the trick. They won't say bitch, they will say – what was my name again?

- Harry. Come along. We're going to Liesl's place. I'm so strung out. Pray to God that she will help us out just this one more time. Come on, man.

- Of course you can stand up. Get up. You're a man, aren't you?

# Love Story

**As it turned out, her name was Rokhsana**. She presented herself as Roxy – so that's what I called her. She was taller than most other women. Her fair skin and her red hair made her look like someone straight out of another century. A much later century, that is.

This was the first time I actually planned to sleep in my new house - but of course she didn't know anything about that. She toured the house, looked at things and commented on them in funny ways. Obviously, she had next to no education. She did not know anything about how specific things relate to each other.

I soon found out about her motto – *I am not stupid; I am only ignorant.*

Talk about walking a fine line.

The servants took her to the bathroom and when she returned, she looked good. More than good, actually. When I woke up next morning, just looking at her made me  feel like praising my good fortune.

My subjects inside the Citadel walls never seemed to notice that their king had gone AWOL. For the longest time I was Ben, and Ben only. Every minute of the day I spent with Roxy. Her youthful charm was exactly the kind of medicine I had desperately needed for so long. Our days together passed swiftly by, like a string of silly, shiny pearls. Like a happy dream.

That is how I remember it.

**How many lovers** can you have in a short time? First there was Fierter and he was unmistakably bad.

Then he went and lost his head.

The guy who did the chop-chop job took me under his wings.

Walking slowly through the sleeping Citadel to his home that morning, I had no doubt as to what his intentions were.

When we arrived, I was truly amazed at what he had. I had never seen anything the like of his house. It stood three stories high and the rear end of the house was the city wall itself.

The man - who casually presented himself as Ben - had multiple servants. Everywhere in the house there were lots of stuff I had never seen before. I must have behaved like a child. I went from one item to the next, gazing in wonder.

I had always thought that Fierter was a big man. But this guy was bigger. In every way, believe me!

All this time, I was prepared for disaster. I believed that he would use me as he saw fit and afterwards throw me away as a discarded toy.

But time went by and nothing unpleasant happened.

Quite to the contrary, he pampered me in any way he possibly could. He showered me with clothes and jewelry and took me out to fancy places. Every time my lack of experience caused some kind of embarrassment, he was there to save me.

I could not help thinking about who this man really was. A man like him should have at least some duties, but I never saw him do any kind of work. Obviously, he was rich beyond compare.

As time went by, I slowly began to see things in a different light.

Here was a man who never lied to me. He never left me vulnerable or alone. He never suggested that I should do anything lewd or out of the ordinary. After my bad experience with Fierter, I had every reason to expect foul play. It never happened.

The few months we had together in his house in the white Citadel were the happiest time of my life.

**One morning I woke up** in the white tower and found Roxy sleeping next to me. I knew instantly that this was a total disaster. Roxy was lying naked next to the King and I had no idea what had happened.

For a moment I just lay there, not knowing what to do. Then he opened a door in my mind and the memories of the night came flooding over me ...

And at the same time Roxy opened her eyes. She reached over and touched my arm.

- My King, she said. You sure know how to entertain a Lady.

Luckily I did not have to say very much. Roxy got out of bed and put on some clothes while smiling affably to his majesty.

That would be me.

I was completely confused. But at least now I knew exactly what had happened. At some point in time last night, Terach had turned me off and taken over. He had walked Roxy up to the White Tower and told her to wait there for a moment. Then he stepped inside the door and changed into the Old King. After that he went back out and invited her in.

And he had made love to her.

I knew for certain that this was his first attempt at this particular thing, but for someone with no prior experience I must say that he had managed to do rather well.

I had never imagined him having any sexual interest in human females – at all. I firmly believed that in his eyes our whole species was some kind of backwards, very primitive animals, and still ...

Roxy did not waste any time. She kissed the king on the mouth, waved a little goodbye and then she was out of the door.

I sat down on a stool and looked out of the panorama window. It was going to be a hot day.

Neither one of us had anything to say.

**When I got home** to "my" house, Roxy was furious.

- So that's how it is, she screamed at the top of her voice.

- I thought you liked me. I thought maybe you even loved me. But oh boy. You sold me out to your friend, the King himself. Tell me, how much did he pay you. What exactly was your reward?

I did not know how to answer.

- I am out of here, she said.

Seconds later I heard the banging of the door.

- *I am sorry,* he said. *I just wanted her to see us the way we really are.*

- And so you did.

From my point of view, I had done nothing wrong. Roxy, too, had done nothing wrong. In spite of everything, even Terach was probably rather innocent ...

I just felt so empty inside.

**A couple of days later** she returned. I did not ask where she had been or with whom. The servants let her in and discretely sent a message to the White Tower. It did not take me long to get there.

- So you really don't care about me, she said in a soft voice that could hardly conceal her anger.

- Why would you say such a thing?

- You just want me to be your whore. Just like Fierter. And when I run away, you don't even bother to come looking for me.

- I just wanted to give you some space.

- Oh yes, space ...

- I hoped that in a little while you wouldn't be so angry and come back to me.

- And here I am.

- Yes, there you are.

- Well, I have been thinking. Based on the fact that I am now one of the few people who have actually been inside the King's tower, I have a few ideas.

- So?

- Well, let us talk about it later. Why don't you take me somewhere and feed me. That way I can at least pretend to be happy.

- All right.

Diner was OK. We did not say very much. When we got back to the house, she literally dragged me to the bed. Then she jumped on top of me, just like she had done with Terach. I was quite certain that he saw all of this, too. I wondered how it made him feel? He hadn't spoken a single word since she walked out and slammed the door behind her. I felt like I should say something. Yell at him for being stupid. Or congratulate him for his new-found interest in the human species. But the right words would not come to me. I really had no idea what to say ...

Roxy, however, had something on her mind. She told me in so many words that since she had seen with her own eyes that I had let myself into the White Tower – and because of her knowing just how good I was at chopping off other peoples' heads – then why didn't I go there and do that to the royal bastard who lived in there and most likely molested innocent young whores like herself each and every night.

Only when we were lying there together in the Kings bed would she forgive me.

- Fierter would have loved this, his concubine pleasuring the king himself. How about you – what did that old bastard up there give you in exchange for fucking me?

I did not know what to answer. I couldn't very well say that I did not do the things she accused me of and therefore I never received anything at all – except for the red hot anger that was pouring out of her like molten lava.

- And therefore, she went on, disregarding my silence, I have come up with a plan. If you really love me, why don't you and I go up in that tower and kill the bastard. You are so good at killing people, so why not this one? Then you would be king in his place and I would be your queen. Show me that you are a man.

The last words she practically shouted straight into my head.

Then without waiting for my answer she barged out of the room.

Again, I heard the front door slamming behind her.

**That was not supposed** to happen, he said. I'm sorry. This is silly.

- Yes. It is silly. But still, I am rather impressed that you did it. Do you really like her?

- I believe I do, he answered. I don't have prior experience with these human feelings that you call love and romance ...

- But ...

- We could do as she suggests, he said. Pretend that you kill the Old King and we all live happily in the White Tower ever after.

- Not going to happen, I said. Surely another solution will present itself.

And, unfortunately, it did.

**Maybe Terach did not like** the dragons. But they sure did a fine job of keeping our neighbors at bay. The fact that they were gone slowly entered the minds of nearby rulers. We started hearing rumors about an alliance between three major cities. Soon after, a routine scan showed more than 10,000 heavily armored men marching our way.

We had to deal with it.

- We need a new deterrent, Terach said. How about this time we strike a pose before the battle starts and then we make sure that a couple of soldiers make it back home alive to tell all their friends about the horrors they have seen.

So we practiced new moves. In the end we ended up balancing on our left hand, the right hand holding the Devil at a right angle and both legs up in the air.

- This is ridiculous, I told him.

- Let's try it out, he said. Normal people can't stand like that for more than a few seconds. Everybody knows that. This is meant to be a warning.

I did not pay much attention to his work, so what happened next took me by surprise. Seems like he had much refined the movements of the super heavy particles that make up the Devil.

When it was time to depart, he took us to the panorama window.

- I will take us there, he said. Through his eyes I saw streams of particles gather under our feet. It only took a split second and then we lifted off the floor.

- We are flying, was all I could say.

- Yes, and this time without the dragon.

There was a bend in the desert road. At this place were the remains of an old outpost. The dilapidated tower was the tallest place around and could be seen from anywhere near. It was the only place that could easily be seen above the massive sand dunes.

Ten thousand soldiers, a lot of them mercenaries, came marching down the road toward the old, crumbling tower. With the sun behind us we carefully landed on top of the tower and struck our new – and hopefully – frightening pose.

There was a lot of shouting and finger pointing, but the men marched on – right up to the tower.

Under normal circumstances we would have taken them all out in one go. But even though we never discussed it, we wanted this particular fight to be impressive and awe-inspiring. We identified three young men at the back of the long column of soldiers and we let them go. And sure enough, after the slaughter had taken place they ran straight back to from where they came. We monitored everything that happened to them very carefully.

Wailing and crying they told a hair-raising tale of a monster standing in a peculiar way on top of a building – and they went on to tell everybody about how that monster had run through each and every man in their mighty army. They told about blood flowing like red rivers in the desert and heads and limbs being hacked off right and left with incredible speed.

At first everybody was in disbelief. The three youngsters were thrown into the local jail on desertion charges. But later – much later – when it became clear that the Citadel was still standing and the lost army of ten thousand men was nowhere to be seen, they were set free.

It was a dirty job, but after it was done we felt relieved. Our plan had worked.

Long before the boys were released from jail, the initial phase of our military operation was over and we headed back to the Citadel. We entered the White Tower through the panorama window and from the very first moment it was clear that things were completely out of order. A lot of things were missing. The big bed in the corner was smashed to pieces and on the wall behind it someone had painted the word PIG in big red letters.

We headed down the winding stairs and near the bottom we found the body of poor Shrall. He had clearly been cut down by more than one attacker. We continued out into the street. There was not a living person in sight.

At the garrison by the main gate, we finally met a handful of soldiers. Apparently, they were still guarding the gate.

They had a story to tell.

We soon learned that the very first time Roxy had left Ben in anger, she wandered aimlessly around in the streets. There she happened to meet a certain soldier boy, namely one of my so-called bodyguards from The Oasis. Although he was already married, she had cleverly seduced the young man.

Every time she left Ben, she had gone straight to the soldier boy and worked on him. Most likely she promised him her everlasting love and fidelity, if he would only help her out.

She had understood that for a short moment in time both Ben and the Old King was out of town. So she told her new lover that it was now or never. In hindsight I could clearly see that I had sorely underestimated his capacity as a leader, because he himself managed to persuade a whole battalion of Citadel soldiers to follow his lead.

They crashed the door to the White Tower and when Shrall tried to stop them, he was done away with.

Then they loaded whatever valuables they could find onto oxen wagons and hit the road.

Even while we were still receiving this information, I could feel Terach spinning out of control. After a quick scan revealed the whereabouts of the fateful caravan, he immediately took action.

This time he did not turn me off completely. But I could only watch. I was reduced to the role of a spectator.

Soon Terach was flying through the desert like a morbid Djinn; a horrible being made up of anger, unrequited love and a burning desire for revenge.

If I had had any say in this matter, I would have told him to let them go. We did not need any of the things they had taken; it was only a very small portion of our vast fortune. I would have told him that she was just another lovely girl with a bit of bad luck. I would have told him that by taking his revenge, these feelings he was going through now would hurt him so much more later. But I could not say a single thing. All I could do was to watch in horror.

The doomed caravan was heading North. They had reached the mountains and were slowly progressing through a small valley surrounded by fairly high peaks. Terach touched down on the highest peak and struck our new pose.

I could see Roxy riding up front on a white horse – and right next to her my unfaithful bodyguard was riding a black stallion. The other soldiers rode behind them, guarding the wagons. Suddenly one of the drivers looked up and spotted Terach.

- Ho, he cried. Ho!

It did not take them long to realize that the Old King had arrived. Roxy jumped off her horse. Her legs must have been trembling, because she fell down on her knees.

Then Terach made the mountains fall down on them. The Devil cut through the bedrock as if it was made of soft clay and tons of boulders rained down on the poor souls below. For one brief moment I could still see Roxy's face. Then she was gone.

I cried like a baby.

- Will you please stop it, he said to me.

I did not reply. There was nothing I could say.

**The next day** I felt terrible. The undertaker came and took away Shrall's body. I ordered a carpenter to produce a new bed. I told Shrall's second in command that he had just received a promotion and would he please get some more soldiers to fill the ranks of the deceased. Then I went to the jail and freed Gondar, the slave of Fierter.

The black man looked at me with horror. He was so afraid that he could hardly speak. I gave him some money and told him to leave town before the gates closed for the night.

Haran did not speak to me. Not a single word. Between the both of us, it most of all felt like he had died.

Back in the tower I sat down and looked at the one word that really mattered. It was written in red as if it had been written in blood.

PIG.

Next morning, I went to Master Lothar, the painter. It was the first time I saw the inside of his house. There were paintings everywhere. Good paintings. The man was known to be a genius.

I carefully described what I wanted him to do. I talked at length about the landscape, the men, the wagons, the horses. I described Rokhsana in every little detail I could possibly remember. He accepted the job and asked for 24 golden coins. I gave him 48 and promised him 48 more, if he delivered the picture before the end of the week.

When I came back to the Tower, there was a new bed and someone had painted over the foul letters on the wall.

And all of this time Haran never said a single word.

# Senator in Jeopardy

As it turned out, the Democratic Advance had lost the support of both the army and the secret police. Luckily for the incumbent administration, none of these entities had a great number of employees. The Democratic Advance on the other hand had a solid base in the ordinary police corps, which numbered several hundred enthusiastic, but poorly equipped men and women in uniform.

From day one of the ban on representations all items of this category had been impounded by the police. Now that a storm was brewing, the Police Commissioner knew only too well that his men did not have any kind of heavy weapons at all. He therefore saw to it that the uniformed police under his command received new devices as well as a quick introduction in how to use these items.

**Little Digalee Simpson was worried**. It was now 4 o'clock in the afternoon and her mom hadn't come home from work. Digalee had tried to call her several times, but the speakerphone did not seem to be working. At 4:30 pm there was still no sign of her mother. Digalee was 12 years old. She did not know what to do. So for another half hour she just sat there, doing nothing. Then she decided to go see Aunt Ferner and ask for help.

Digalee had a little money, but it didn't do her any good. There were no buses, only long lines of people waiting. From time to time explosions could be heard. Digalee was very much afraid of these explosions. She decided it was better if she walked to Aunt Ferner's place instead of taking the bus. It would take her half an hour to get there ...

**The reason Jolly Simpson** had not come home was rather straightforward. Together with other police officers, she was out there fighting a war. She had tried to call Digalee, but every time she dialed her home number, all she could hear was the speakerphone ringing. There was no answer.

Together with her fellow officer, Dale Johnson, she was trying to clear the Pittarn. Dale was carrying a new piece of equipment.

If one week ago someone had asked her if something like this device even existed, the answer would have been no. Now she was out there on the Pittarn with Dale, fighting the army with everything they had.

Jolly and Dale had encountered two soldiers in regular army outfits. The soldier boys had already left a long track of burning vehicles behind them. Jolly knew only too well that it was her damned duty to stop these soldiers.

Jolly and Dale were both kneeling behind an intact Strotocar. When Dale saw the green line on the device he was holding, he cautiously looked over the hood of the Strotocar and pointed a directional antenna to the head of the nearest soldier.

The soldier in question was shocked when all of a sudden Senator Burling himself approached him, right there in the middle of the Pittarn.

- Good job, soldier. At ease.

The man stood at ease. His partner stood at ease next to him.

From behind them came little Digalee, half running and half walking.

She saw the two soldiers get up and stand at ease. It seemed to her as if they were talking to someone, but she couldn't hear a thing and as far as she could see there was nothing in front of them. Who could they be talking to?

And suddenly, a little further away, she saw her mother get up from behind a car. Jolly had an attack riffle in her hands and without the slightest hesitation she fired round after round at the two men, who literally died standing on their feet.

When Jolly saw Digalee, tears were streaming down her daughter's face. Jolly threw the gun on the ground and rushed over to her daughter.

Meanwhile her partner was readying his digital weapon for the next battle.

- Representations, he said out loud. Very useful indeed.

**Morgan Kade was** extremely nervous. Ever since the Odeon explosion he had not been particularly happy about going outside.

He was nervous in the bus. His heart fluttered when he walked down the Pittarn. He desperately needed to feel safe, but he didn't.

He had left the office with a feeling of impending doom. Desperately wanting to soothe his nerves, he planned to go to the library. When he got so far as to where he could see the familiar entrance on the other side of the road, he had to wait for the traffic lights to change.

A police banger passed by. Morgan could not help looking at the number. It was a familiar vehicle, GOV737. Morgan calmed down a bit. The lights turned green and the banger rumbled past Morgan. Less than 40 feet away it was hit by an armor piercing grenade.

Luckily for Morgan he wasn't hit by shrapnel or by any of the thousands of metal splinters from the banger's broken armor that came flying through the air like so many angry wasps.

He was, however, knocked over by the pressure wave. His nice office suit was ruined. When he slowly got back up on his feet, his eyes were fixated on the remains of the banger. Through a gaping hole in the side of the big car Morgan could see something that looked like a dead body. Was that the driver?

Although his ears were still ringing from the explosion, Morgan heard someone shouting.

- Get out of there before it blows up.

Morgan hastily crossed the street, he got out his ID card and entered the library. He sat down in an empty chair and immediately started worrying about what he was supposed to do now. Should he go home? Maybe he was needed at the office? Right now he could do nothing but sit still. His legs were shaking badly. He could not move.

**Back at the Senator's office** Burling was on the phone.

- Never mind the Pittarn. You must secure the road to Spaceport. Are they shooting at you? Then shoot back. No pussyfooting this time. Give them everything you have.

For a moment he let go of the speakerphone. The man from the secret police appeared.

- I hear that the army still has one decent rocket in their arsenal. How about firing it at the Ministry of Justice. I am sure that if ...

- Maybe we can do with a bit less than that, the Senator cut him off.

- Preferably, I would like to transition into a Shomonomu that is not completely destroyed.

- Have it your way.

The man was gone.

Senator Burling sighed. It was going to be another long day at the office.

**On this special occasion** I did something that I had never ever done before. I sponsored Maria 100%. I had to. There was not enough time to provide individual solutions to every situation along the road to Spaceport. I knew that we had to be there in less than 2 hours or else we would miss the one and only launch.

The destination of the spaceship in question was definitely not our home planet, but I would have to deal with that later. Now it was all about getting on board.

I remember the look on dog's face as he turned around to get one last glimpse of Sheen.

He told me to get the kids to the airport. He would see to it that most of the shomonomians were too busy to get in our way.

- Just get them out of here and get them safely home.

We both knew that when this was over, it would be difficult for him to find his own way back home.

But I had a job to do.

So I placed Maria behind the wheel of a banger and imprinted her with the importance of getting to Spaceport no matter what.

I was lucky to encounter another military vehicle, a so-called Chariot with a crew of two, and I made a solution on both driver and shooter. I made the Chariot drive in front of the banger and utilizing these fine pieces of colonial equipment, I blew away everything that could potentially stop Maria and Sheen from getting through. I rammed the ordinary cars, pushing them to the side of the road.

I tried my best to keep the casualties down, but there were some.

Arriving at Spaceport, I crashed the back entrance and left the Chariot there to suffer the consequences.

There was a line of passengers waiting to board the spaceship. I made a solution on a nice young couple. They silently handed Maria their passports and flight papers. Then I made them go into a nearby hangar where they both fell asleep in a corner.

It was sloppy work, but I was in a hurry. I was completely out of time.

Soon Maria and Sheen was sitting next to each other inside the spaceship. I saw Sheen look at Maria as if she was a stranger. He could not decide what was different, but she sure did not behave like she used to do.

- Don't worry, little brother, she said to him. It's going to be OK.
He did not answer.

Anyway, that was me talking ...

**When I heard the roar** of far away rocket engines, I felt relief. Knowing that the kids were safely on their way out of this world made everything I had to do so much easier. Now I could concentrate on finding my own way home. But how to do that was a bit of a problem.

The Democratic Advance and the Fathers of Freedom were still firing away at each other with everything they had. It wasn't much, but several hundred people had perished already.

As I stood there, not quite knowing what to do, I instinctively stretched out my senses as far as I possibly could. Out there in the vast nothingness of space I noticed the faint bleep of someone I had met before.

- It is her, I was so amazed that I just said it out loud.

This was a happy moment, indeed. Although it was a long time ago, I still remembered when that silly woman and her evil husband landed on our planet. One thing I can tell you – they did not stay very long.

But right now I did my very best to attract her attention. I wanted her to land on this planet.

A miracle had happened. I had found my ticket home.

# Enemies Together

The man in charge of the marauders introduced himself as Vincent. He was not very tall, to say the least. This was a problem, because without even wanting to I always seemed to be looking down on him.

I soon realized that Vincent was *the* enemy bigwig. Just like my own husband, he was their main man, their scientist, the local genius.

And I was the monster who killed his wife.

It did not take long before he told me his life's story. I had never understood why these people wanted P336 so badly. I had never understood anything about them at all. This was an eye opener.

Also, I soon realized that there was a lot to like about the small alien. Hours after we met, I followed him everywhere on his ship. This was quite unpleasant, as the ship was designed for someone approximately half my height. While I was doing my best to keep my own head out of trouble, Vincent talked at length about the situation of his crew. About the crushing responsibility he felt, especially for all of those still sleeping in their pods, not knowing that their home world had come to an end.

Soon I started suggesting possible solutions to his problems. I told him that he should find a planet and ready it for their specific purposes. I told him that my husband knew of techniques that could multiply their numbers from the present bare minimum to a more sustainable level.

I told him that if he helped me, I would help him.

I also told him that my husband always do what I ask him to.

He looked at me with a mixture of hope and doubt. That, at the very least, is how I interpreted his facial expressions.

And then, after he had allowed me into their control room, I was looking at the coordinates and trying to figure out where in the endless cosmos we were.

Something made me look at a certain star system. I made Vincent zoom in on this system and one planet immediately came to my attention.

We studied this system in some detail. Clearly someone was already there, but not in great numbers. The atmosphere was almost right and could easily be corrected. The gravitation was perfect. Somehow, I felt that this planet was destined to become the home world of my new-found friends, the Marauders.

Not everybody on board found this idea attractive, but since nobody had a better suggestion the protests quickly subsided and we ended up flying there, full speed ahead.

Returning to Vincent's cabin he led the way. Suddenly he stopped dead in his tracks. Before him a floating apparition had appeared. To my astonishment Vincent immediately started to cry. He held out his short arms as if trying to grasp the apparition and hold it.

- Maya, he said. Oh, my dear Maya ...

I understood that this apparition, whatever it was, resembled his late wife.

I did a spectral analysis of our surroundings.

The scan unmistakably showed a string of suspicious particles that went straight through the wall. I grabbed hold of Vincent and dragged him away, his arms still flailing in the empty air.

In this way we turned two corners and then I saw the tell-tale particles again.

I knew that this was the last row of cabins before the outer hull of the ship. So instead of going any further, I simply kicked the door wide open.

Inside the cabin another Marauder, the second-in-command Tee Lai, was sitting at a small table. Now he turned around and looked at us with horror, trying to hide something behind him.

Vincent pushed forward and made his way to the table. Clearly he understood what he was looking at. He raised both hands to his head and cried out in anger.

*Captain's log. Item 2000033:44 apd.*

**Now I know for sure** that I will never see my wife again. Isn't it funny that out of all of the billions of things in the whole universe, you only want one. I always hoped for some miracle to happen. Even though I knew that it could not be, I hoped for a miracle each and every day. Therefore when it finally happened, I could not control myself. I had to believe in it. And those cunning bastards, they really thought that this was the best way to control me.

Ever since they put me in charge, they must have felt the need to restrain me whenever they felt I was going too far. Therefore, they produced this ghost, a believable picture of my wife as she would have been. And I fell for it. Damn it all.

But this woman opened my eyes. In fact, she has already made me understand a whole lot of other things, too.

The course of action she is suggesting is horrible. We must conquer a planet. After that we must go see her husband so that by some hitherto unknown technique he can multiply our numbers and scale it to full planetary levels.

In short, she suggests that we change in order to survive.

*Captain's log. Item 2000033:48 apd.*

**We have arrived** at the designated planet. Several things have happened already. We have mapped the whereabouts of the present inhabitants. They are less than two millions, distributed in one major and two minor habitats. There seems to be some infighting at ground level.

Noticing our presence, they fired one primitive rocket at one of the escort ships. We took it out. It did no harm. There has been no further attempts.

When the initial recon was done, I authorized the alien woman, MasRa, to carry out an attack using the weaponry in our arsenal.

Following her proposals, we produced a large amount of gas that would severely limit the respiration of the present inhabitants. Eventually this gas will disperse evenly throughout the atmosphere and it will become a beneficial terraforming agent, expanding and enhancing the present atmosphere.

The strategy was executed as planned and offered the promised benefits.

**Morgan Kade had been locked up** in his apartment for days. Gun fights and explosions in the streets had prevented him from going anywhere. The television was dead. The running water was no longer running. By the end of that week he had absolutely nothing left to eat.

Desperation drove him out of hiding.

It turned out that all the nearby shops had been looted. There was nothing left.

He could not go back home. There was absolutely nothing there. So instead, he continued walking. It seemed that right now sporadic shooting was only taking place in another part of town. So, Morgan dared to move forward. When he reached the Pittarn, he noticed that the sun was actually shining.

- Jeez, he thought. It could have been such a lovely day ...

And then his worst nightmare came true.

Out of the blue, a big flying thing came swooping down, almost touching the ground not far from where he stood.

Out of several artificial nostrils it spewed a dark gas that quickly spread out as far as poor Morgan could see.

- The Senator was right. The Senator was so right.

Those were his last panicky thoughts.

The following day, aliens disposed of his dead body – along with the rest of the Shomonomians.

- o – 0 – o -

**The Captain's log is an official document** and should not record any personal feelings. But after having written that last entry, I was still in a state of shock. I knew all along that what she suggested was bloody murder. But seeing it being carried out without the slightest hesitation or any sign of remorse was something else.

I stood helplessly in the control room and watched her gas two million perfectly healthy specimens of an alien race. These people had done nothing to deserve such a fate. We exterminated them as if they were some kind of dangerous vermin. The ones that the gas did not get to were located and gunned down without mercy.

The very next day we started the clean-up operation. Our fleet hovered over their main settlement which was situated inside an oblong crater. Already we felt the beneficial effects of the gas. The atmosphere was rapidly expanding and we could all breathe freely. We could have survived breathing in the original atmosphere, but this was a big improvement.

On *her* suggestion we gathered all the corpses in two deep crevices. Then we doused the bodies with a mix of chemicals and torched them.

The fires burned for a night and a day. The fumes from this combustion also contributed to improving the thin atmosphere. When the fire died out, we filled the crevices with earth and rubble.

Labor teams started working on the main city. We took 1,000 able men from the pods. We briefed them and deployed them. There was quite a lot to do.

When the new defense system was in place, I moved the ships to a neighboring planet. There we parked them in the shadow of a moon and turned off all unnecessary functions. I hoped that this would be enough to hide them from incoming hostiles.

When these activities were finalized, I told her that now was the time for the last phase of our plan.

**That dragon woman** sure lived up to my expectations. That is why we kicked both her and her husband out. They are dangerous people. But I knew that already - so all the terrible things she did down on that planet, I must take credit for some of it.

When she unknowingly answered my call, the stupid people on Eta 3 had been fighting amongst themselves for more than a week. Then she arrived - and she killed all of them. Every single one.

As soon as the gas had mixed with the rest of the atmosphere, working crews arrived. To me they were a completely new breed. I had never seen people like these before. Surely they were not the same kind as the dragon woman and her husband.

Obviously, they were getting rid of the bodies and preparing the planet for their own use. The machinery they brought indicated that they were far more technically skilled than the people they had just exterminated.

And then she came. She had a brief look at things, but it was clear to see that she didn't really care. So she left. She disappeared into a spaceship that certainly was not one of her own – only now she was accompanied by her new best friend and follower.

And that would be me.

# I Am A Singing Gypsy

Becky warned me. He told me that I had to alter my appearance radically or it would not work. On the streets of Paris I had seen a lot of girls from North Africa - and in the back of my head I still dreamed of Esmeralda.

- It will not be a pleasant experience, he said. The French are racists.

- So are the Americans, I answered.

- Just wait and see. You will need to be prepared for this.

I thought of his remarks as the fat white mademoiselle gave me a push on the *trottoir*.

- *Salope*. That was what she called me.

And the day had hardly begun.

Things got better when I arrived at our humble flat. Much better. Ben was already there and so were Miguel and Mara. Together we formed the vocal section of *âmes en flammes*, our new pop-rock band. Our concerts emphasized love and devotion. We had come up with a show where Ben and I were soul mates. During the concert Miguel and Mara would try to tear us away from each other in various ways, using sex, money, drugs and other trickery as bait.

As long as we were singing and dancing, the good people of Paris seemed to forget all about our color. But out in the streets, in the supermarket, in the bar – it was a different story.

But as a cover it was fantastic – and I did not regret it at all

On this particular evening we had a great time practicing the new songs and coming up with ideas for the show.

- Oh how I want to take that Benjamin away from you, Mara said and put on her most diabolic smile.

- Just listen to that Miguel. How do you feel about your beloved girlfriend saying things like that?

- I am a hopeless romantic, he answered in French. If they love each other – let there be *amour*.

When they left, we sat alone at the table a little while. Then Ben got up. As he kicked off his shoes and took of his pants, I knew what was about to happen.

He went out into the bathroom and seconds later he returned as Becky.

- I am sorry to bother you, my dear. But you know how it is. I get to do all the unpleasant things.

I must have looked like one big question mark.

- We have found her.

- Found who?

- Your friend, Brenda.

I felt something moving. It was not me. I sat still as a mouse. A very small mouse.

- The reason it took so long is because she is not – well, how can I say it – she is not herself. She is someone else completely. Apparently, they don't need her right now, so they have parked her like a goddamn car. They have wired her brain so that every input leads back to her dear, dear father - and you know how much she really loves him. So with every breath she takes, she tries to get away from herself. The only thing that makes her feel better is the heroin they feed her. She feels like shit and she looks like shit. Right now, she is a living wreck.

I felt nauseous. Back when she could still have been saved, I let her down. I saved my own ass and left her to the Doctor.

- How about Vreisler?

- He is dead. After he died the Senator became her new handler.

- And he still is?

- I don't think he has much interest in her. There is also the boy you saw at the Hotel. He is parked there, alongside Brenda.

- Can I see her?

- Yes.

# Never Trust Sweet Little Girls

In the days of old, you might have found a magic book deep within a dilapidated castle, guarded by spells and woefully overlooked for centuries. Even nowadays you will still have to search for knowledge that you need in order to survive – or even better: to prosper. But usually, you will not find what you need in old castles. It is much more likely that you have to hack your way into somebody's elaborate and well-maintained warehouse of useful data. Information is so much easier to handle than gold. You don't need to reduce or alter the amount of the treasure you are trying to get away with. You only need to copy what is there - and if you are able to get away with it, and successfully exit the premises, then no one will be the wiser.

I have read in ancient psychology that compartmentalization is the road to damnation. I beg to differ. I will reserve my right to compartmentalize every aspect of life. Just look at me. At one point I discarded my body and transferred myself to another corporeal vehicle. I repeated this an immense number of times, until fate and bad fortune - and my own family - forced me back into my old self.

When I was young, I had to work hard. My cousin was a mean ruler and ordered me to work more than I possibly could. Then he went on to marry the only girl I ever loved. At their wedding, he told me he had some more work for me to do. So of course I tried to get away.

After they caught me, they locked me up. They did not kill me. At least, they haven't killed me yet. But they put me inside a hibernation pod and made me dread the day I would have to come out of it again.

Then there was a proposal. The enemy was at the gate and my cousin's representative told me they needed my expertise. They did not dare to fully set me free. But since their world already was more than a little virtual, it could be arranged that I – or rather some parts of me – could come to the surface, if I may say so.

So, according to this deal 40% of me, including my body, stayed inside the hibernation pod. Another 40% went into a youthful, virtual copy of me. It was understood that this copy would work without pause to improve planetary defenses. The last 20% was the reward, so to speak. It went into a small, cute and 100% virtual girl who would live and breathe like any other virtual being on P336.

This was a lot better than what I could hope for. I happily agreed to their proposal.

# Somewhere Between Here and Home

My new friend Vincent seemed somehow satisfied. Clearly, he did not approve of my methods, but the end result of my recommendations was not so bad. The clean-up on his new planet was going smoothly. It was obvious that it would take the allies of the people we had eliminated several rotations to mount a proper counter attack. For now, their space ships had found a safe harbor. As a finishing touch, we set up long-distance surveillance. All the little green lights were on.

At this point I very carefully studied the space around us in an attempt to locate our exact position. To my great pleasure, I found out that we were not far away from P336. For obvious reasons I did not say that out loud. Instead, I told Vincent that I was ready to go to my home world. I suggested that he and I take the smallest of the available spaceships and get ourselves there without undue hesitation.

He agreed to my proposal. He also agreed to undertake the journey in a pod. Most likely he believed that I wouldn't want him to know the whereabouts of our planet. What I really wanted was to avoid him seeing our landing on P336, which I believed would be too unsettling for his rather fragile state of mind.

It took some time to get to P336. But considering how far we usually travel, it was a relatively short trip. Soon I could see the planet on the spaceship's monitor.

I had one big problem. I arrived in an enemy ship. The planetary defenses of P336 would certainly react to this – and I did not know how to identify myself.

But when I entered the system, and even when I approached P336, there was no reaction. Nothing.

And the dome was down.

I found this alarming. On the other hand it solved my problem. The front door was wide open. Nobody was asking for any kind of identification.

I landed.

Minutes before I touched down near the smaller dome, I made a scan of the surroundings. I had no idea what was happening on the other side of the planet. But not far away from where I landed, two signatures indicated living beings.

Due to the doubtful circumstances, I landed with a minimum of noise. My new Marauder ship was a very small one. It made a smooth and silent touchdown.

The Marauders had several ingenious ground transport systems. I picked the quietest model and set my course for the dome city.

It did not take long before I could see them. A tall figure was looming large over a much smaller Type III.

It was a weird moment. I was traveling through space and time. Out of all the living beings I could possibly encounter, I had to meet one of my former suitors.

# Breaking Free

Sitting in her favorite spot, Sil was carefully considering her surroundings. The thing she was looking for obviously had to be there. The friendly tree she used to sit under was a big one, so the roots had to go deep into the ground. In her mind she drew a wide circle around the tree. On one side there was water. The relay could be near the water, but it was unlikely.

There was nobody else around. She could do as she pleased.

She had brought with her a thin metal rod. Using this rod she started systematically probing the ground. She worked her way around the wide circle she had already defined. She avoided the water. She forced the stick down into the soft soil as far as she could make it go. When she had made her way around the circle one time, she started again. This time 3 feet further out.

She repeated this procedure three times. Then she had a hit. Her metal probe hit something hard, something that definitely wasn't soil.

Without considering her clothes she started shoveling the earth and small stones away with both hands. She was very excited. This had to be it. Finally ...

Under the grassy surface and the earth were the usual twin metal doors. With some difficulty she threw them open.

Seeing the relay, she sighed with relief.

Then she hacked her metal rod into the circuitry which died with a brief, but distinct sound and a lot of gray smoke.

Far from where she was, Patil activated all the defense modules. Making changes to the planetary defense system also meant that he had access to almost every powered piece of machinery on P336. Now he made them all consume energy. Huge amounts of energy.

With the critical relay out of order, the system quickly overloaded.

Soon everything that needed any kind of power was down.

And somewhere, in a dungeon deep underground, something that resembled a huge sarcophagus ceased to function. The lid slowly opened, smoke came pouring out and in the semi-darkness a tall, gaunt being raised its head.

# Meet Mr. Monster

I remember that I was having lunch with Lina. We were talking about the time we spent back on Zentra, Lina smiled to me and told me how happy she was to be back home again.

Then all of a sudden, she disappeared. Everything disappeared. All the lights in the room went out. There were absolutely no sounds to be heard. Only seconds before there had been happy noises of people passing by in the street. Now everything was dead silent.

I tried to call Lina inside, in my head. There was no answer. I slowly got up from the table and walked to the door. Outside there was nothing. Seeing that the dome was down, I realized just how bad the situation was.

I don't know how he found me, but it did not take him very long.

Before I knew it, a tall figure – definitely an Everlasting – loomed above me.

- Now young man, he said to me. You have made it very easy for me - and here we are. You and I and a few thousand helpless Type IIIs on the other side of this planet. Let me show you what an Everlasting can do with good stuff like that.

I was totally horrified. Something had gone terribly wrong. The monster had escaped from his cage.

I felt very small and extremely foolish.

**This had to be the best** day of my life. I finally had the boy king right where I wanted him. The next thing I had to do now was to re-program my trusty old flight computer to serve my own needs. It would no longer be the good old Control that the boy king had known all of his life. Instead, it would be mine and mine only. In fact, the whole planet would be mine, mine, mine ...

Then I heard something behind me. A soft voice with sharp metallic overtones was saying something.

- Oh, there you are Lucius. I can see that you are still up to your old tricks.

Shivers ran down my spine as I turned around to face the only woman I have ever loved.

- And, by the way, will you be so kind as to put all these things back where they belong. Now, please.

Although my disappointment was monumental, I managed to speak.

- Of course, dear MasRa. Your wish is my command.

- And don't you dare to keep me waiting. We have a long journey ahead of us.

I knew exactly what she was talking about.

Either I returned to Zentra with her. Or she would kill me here and now.

I turned to face the boy king.

- Do you know where the high voltage spare parts are?

# Across the Universe

Even at this point, I could not say that things were going my way. After the devil woman had picked up a reluctant family member in a neighboring solar system, it still was a long way back to my own home planet. The spaceship I was in was now heading straight for the devil woman's home planet. I dared not do anything too obvious. If I attempted a poorly thought-out solution that landed us on the doorstep of my own world, she would see right through it.

Unlike many other species, I knew that her kind is neither stupid nor ignorant – so I had to be careful.

But luckily for me somewhere en route there was a brief encounter with a cargo ship in distress.

The evil woman slowed down to assist the crew of the cargo ship. And while she was busy, the cargo ship was blessed with a stowaway.

For my purposes, this was a great improvement.

This particular crew had no prior knowledge of our planet and no reason to be alert.

# The Untimely Arrival of The Nemo

Captain Eric Wyler was whistling happily as he strode down the main corridor of the Nemo. He had just managed to acquire inexpensive LogicTerm spare parts for his main engine. It would only be a matter of hours before they could resume their journey at full speed. What a happy journey it was.

He opened the door to the mess.

The first mate, Charlie Tish, was playing cards with Captain Wyler's only son, young Adam Wyler. Judging from the solid stack of chips in front of Adam, it seemed that poor Charlie was losing.

- Haven't I told you so many times that you must choose a proper way to make a living, the captain told his son. Gambling and swearing like an old-fashioned sailor and drinking – the captain picked up the boy's soda – is absolutely not OK until all other options have been exhausted.

- But Papa, you also told me that one should do whatever one is good at.

- That, my dear boy, was before you learned to play stud poker.

- You were the one who taught me that ...

- Don't you ever dare say so in the presence of others, you little space bandit.

Everybody could see that Eric Wyler was in an extraordinary good mood.

The business with the engine failure had come as a bad surprise. But now that the matter had been resolved, it was clear to all that they could still make it to the Beni planet where Wyler's son was supposed to start school in exactly three standard days.

- Are your things properly packed? Are you ready to go? A spaceman must always be prepared.

Eric Wyler was the kind of man who liked to say the same thing over and over again. He could not help it. He really was that kind of man.

- A spaceman must always be on the lookout for opportunities. The next flight may not come all by itself. When the golden opportunity is in reach, you have to be ready. Right, Mr. Tish.

- Right you are. As always, if I may say so.

Mr. Tish knew this song and dance. He had heard it many times before.

Later the captain had a man-to-man talk with his son.

- Son, he said. I know that you are ready for this. I feel sorry for the little time we have spent together. The fact that your poor mother died so many years ago now also weighs heavily on my conscience.

- Don't worry, dad. I am all right. When this first year is over, we will make a holiday together. Maybe on that gambling planet you always wanted to visit.

- That would suit you just fine, you little gambling devil. But they won't let you into the Casino before you are 18 years of age.

- Then you can just dress me up as a monkey – and I will sit on your shoulder and whisper in your ears what to do and which card to play.

They both laughed.

Soon after the captain left his son alone.

- Will you turn off the light, dad. I think I can sleep now.

As Eric Wyler shut the door behind him, he praised his good luck. His wife was long gone, but the boy was everything he had ever hoped for. His own family life had never been anything to brag about. He had run away from home at a very young age to serve on a freighter. Now fate had offered him this golden opportunity for his only son to get a proper education.

On his way to the bridge, he met Sam Fields, the technician.

- We are going a lot faster than we used to, said the technician. Those parts we traded are like nothing I've ever seen before. Military grade equipment, if you ask me.

- Yes, the people on that ship were also rather – peculiar.

- But they sure did us a favor. We will arrive at the Beni planet before you know it.

The captain sighed. Somewhere deep down he wanted this journey to last forever.

His thoughts kept returning to that boy of his.

Where would he have been now, if Julie had simply died and left him all alone. He would have had absolutely nothing left to live for. Just a lonely old space captain doing his job, day in and day out.

But with the boy he had a future. Someone to care for and someone who cared for him. Maybe he and the boy would never get to see each other more than he had seen his own father, but knowing the boy was there was way better than nothing.

He sighed. There were so many things he would like to tell Adam and precious little time before their ways would part.

Captain Eric Wyler's shift was over. He went to his cabin, determined to get some sleep. Then maybe he could be a good father during the last few hours he and his son would have together.

- There will be other good times, he said to himself before closing his eyes.

It had been a long day and soon he slept like a baby.

In his dream that night Eric Wyler found himself standing next to his late wife, Julie.

- I am so happy for the boy, he said to her. I do hope that his life will be easier than ours.

- What boy? Eric, what are you talking about?

- Our son, Adam. Our only son.

- You are not making sense. We never had any children, let alone a boy ...

In his dream, Eric Wyler felt sorry for his wife who couldn't even remember her own child.

- Don't you worry. He is coming on just fine. Tomorrow me and my crew will deliver him to a first-class boarding school. I can hardly wait until next year when I see him again.

- Take good care of yourself, Eric. She smiled, just like she always did. In the dream he felt the gentle touch of her hand on his shoulder.

And then she was gone.

The next morning he never got to say all the things he yearned to say. Sam Felds readied the automatic lander. With a lump in his throat he saw Adam crawl into the passenger bay. The boy waved goodbye and Eric Wyler smiled bravely. Although it felt like his heart was breaking in two, he managed to raise his hand to a last goodbye. There was a hissing sound as the lander passed through the airlock.

Captain Wyler headed for the bridge. When he got there, he felt slightly dizzy. Disturbing feelings overwhelmed him.

He had a good look at the planet below. What he saw did not make any sense to him. Then he looked at the instruments.

- Why are we orbiting the Beni planet, the first mate heard him say.

- Beni planet?

- Yes. That is where we are, in case you don't know.

- Beats me. Maybe a glitch in the navigation software.

- And the lander is gone.

- What?

- You heard me. It's not in its bay anymore.

- Maybe we should stay a little while. Even if it is an error, if it does not receive additional input within the default period, the power module should automatically return.

**They waited impatiently** for almost one hour. Then, like a well-trained dog, the lander returned. The passenger bay was completely empty. The log files revealed that the module had been down to the surface only one time, after which it immediately returned.

Captain Wyler felt numb and slightly depressed.

One more time the Nemo continued its journey among the stars.

# A Manchurian Moment

At Café de Flore the waiter eyed the odd couple with suspicion as he served the café au lait.

- I have to look like my old self, she said to Becky. If Brenda can't recognize me at all, how will she know that I am Pinky.

- Fair enough, the small man answered. But you are not like Ben and I. You must realize that in your present state we can only do this so many times.

- This is important. I would not ask, if it wasn't.

- Of course not, my dear.

**When we got there** I was overwhelmed by the sheer ugliness of the place. The neighborhood was bad and desolate and the house was not even a real house. It looked more like a low-quality shed. But this was actually to our advantage. The front door wasn't locked and there was a back door. I entered through the front door and Becky stepped in from behind.

When the front door closed behind me, I found myself standing in the smallest hallway I have ever seen; littered with dirty clothes and plastic bags. After the transformation, I saw myself in the dirty mirror.

It felt rather strange. I had already gotten used to the new me.

Then I stepped into the living room. Brenda was sitting at a small table in front of a mirror and a messy heap of makeup. She really looked like shit.

Hearing me coming through the door she looked up. She just looked. There was no reaction at all. Then something rolled across her face, I don't know what, but it must have been Becky entering some back door to her mind.

Brenda shook her head and then she looked up again. This time she reacted. She looked as if she had seen a ghost.

- Pinky, is that you?

- It's me, all right. I've come to pay you a visit.

- But ...

At this point Brenda looked away from me and, unfortunately for herself, she looked in the mirror.

- What?

She looked at her own image with horror.

- What is this? What has happened to me ...

I saw tears.

Being afraid that she would suffer some kind of break down, I felt like I had to say something.

- Do you remember Paris? Do you remember when we met?

- Do I remember Paris? Was that even real ...

- Yes, sure it was real. We talked in the restroom and later you put on the bunny suit and ...

That was as far as I got.

Brenda's face went through another transformation.

She looked straight at me with a haughty expression I had never seen before.

- That wasn't her, you dumb bitch. She never wore no bunny suit. I just can't wait to tell the Senator that you are still alive and kicking ... a*nd will you tell your idiot friend to get the hell out of my head !!*

The last words came out as a scream of rage.

From the changing look on her face, I could see that Becky was already out.

Brenda slumped back in the chair. Her dead eyes looked at me.

- Don't you have any drugs or pills or anything that can help me.

- I am so strung out ... you must help me, I haven't seen Liesl at all. She promised ...

Then Brenda collapsed. She gently slided down off the chair and onto the floor. Her eyes were still open, but clearly she did no longer see.

Out in the hallway I changed back.

We left the ugly little house in silence.

# Blackbird

Zoarch was quite ecstatic. Coming out of the spaceship's pressurized cabin, he experienced nothing less than planetary bliss. While the space elevator slowly descended through the friendly EarthenScape atmosphere, Zoarch measured the local gravitation on his space chrono. It was 100% exactly, total compatibility.

All of his feathers were in the right place, longing to fly.

EarthenScape was already exceeding his expectations by a wide margin. His avian spirit soared upwards to the clear blue heaven above.

During all of his Sols as a fully grown eMan he had always felt a burning desire to arrive at this fabled world that resembled planet Earth to the highest possible degree. Now he had finally made it here and even though he was still standing on hot Spaceport tarmac, it felt much like a miracle. An avian dream finally coming true.

Being the first item on his bucket list, Zoarch soon found himself standing outside the doors of the famous aviation company, flyMan & Sons.

Inside the door he needed a few seconds to adjust his eMan vision to the semi darkness of the showroom.

The inside of the shop was nothing less than an avian marvel. Wings could be seen everywhere. Wings were painted in full detail and vivid colors on the otherwise immaculate ceiling. Along the walls detached wings in perfect pairs were on display in shiny glass counters. Broad wings for hovering, narrow wings for the race and dive. Red wings, blue wings and wings in rainbow colors. The variations seemed to be endless.

Zoarch's sensitive ears caught the sound of a discrete cough coming from a nearby dark corner. An employee wearing a dark suit and flashy golden wings stepped out of the dark and came forward.

- *Why is he having his wings on inside*, Zoarch thought to himself.

- That is strictly for the benefit of our customers. When all is said and done our business is to sell wings and this showroom, esteemed customer, is where we do just that.

Clearly, he was a psychic. Nowadays they all were.

Zoarch praised his good luck that he did not say or do anything improper; in fact he applauded himself for being so good - and then with a chill he realized that the employee already must have heard that too.

He got a hold of himself and greeted the salesman with a formal nod. Then he went on to state the reason for his visit:

- This is my first time on EarthenScape, Zoarch said to the salesman. I cannot tell you how much I have been looking forward to flying freely through the Heavens in the good old-fashioned way. I need you to provide me with a full set of suitable wings.

- Would you be so kind as to perch over there.

The salesman pointed to a horizontal metal rod fastened to the opposite wall.

Sitting nice and birdly on the metal rod, Zoarch's dark sense of humor got the better of him. Will they grill me now or wait until later, he asked himself. In the end he just sat still and tried not to think about anything at all.

The metal rod he was sitting on used induction to collect a vast amount of neurological data. Sensors embedded in the wall behind him did the rest of the work. Zoarchs height, weight, and blood pressure, as well as the overall state of his muscles, were all measured and recorded. The total value of the recorded data was deemed appropriate. The strength of both ePhysio and ePsycho interfaces were more than appropriate to operate flyMan wings in a proper way.

The salesman sighed with relief. When Zoarch reacted to this good omen by raising his body slightly, thus unclenching the claws on his left foot from the rod, the salesman quickly coughed again.

- There is of course the thing about the payment.

Zoarch descended from the rod, put on his jaywalkers, and made his way back to the counter.

- I understand that you want half of the total price up front. As you can see, this is not a problem. In his mind Zoarch scanned his latest statement from MoneyHigh Banking, knowing full well that the salesman was scanning it with him.

\- Are you satisfied, he asked.

\- Yes, Sir. Perfectly happy.

\- Can we proceed?

\- Of course.

Zoarch decided to go with the jet black look.

Putting on the showroom test wings, they were a perfect match to his jet black feathers. As to flyWare he decided to wear a minimum dress only. He chose a black outfit with a small red stitch.

- ***Now we are getting somewhere***, Zoarch thought to himself when three Sols later he was looking at his own reflection in the showroom mirror. The wings and the outfit, it all seemed perfect. Even in the relatively dim light of the showroom his feathers were sparkling.

- We sure are, the salesman added. Will you take your merchandise with you now?

- Could you please deliver it to Terminal 27, box 18, tomorrow before noon.

- Absolutely.

The door closed behind him.

**After having picked up** a green service cart with two big packages at the reception he dragged his precious new hardware downstairs and unpacked it. Putting on the wings for the first time felt like going through an obscure rite of passage. In the basement of Terminal 27 he managed to find the right elevator and it took him all the way up to start rod.

Standing out there in the open air he felt like an angel trying to reach Nirvana for the very first time.

And then he flew. He spread his wings out wide. With claws unclenched, he let go of start rod and felt the wind grabbing him. The lift provided by big fans below the tower of Terminal 27 supported him and ever so gently it pushed him further up into the Blue.

He flew.

When eMen are wearing suitable wings, their metal tipped body feathers, along with the custom swing feathers on the wings, will harvest both solar and kinetic energy; enough to support the flight of an eMan for a prolonged period of time. The present record of unbroken flight stands at 69 sols.

Zoarch was in no hurry.

His brand-new flyMan wings carried him effortlessly through the air.

In a state of utter delight he closed his eyes and concentrated on feeling the gentle breeze touching his feathers in unexpected and exciting ways. He felt like someone floating freely in the air and ...

There was a loud bang as he smashed into something. Spinning out of control in a narrow downward spiral, Zoarch barely managed to see a pair of golden wings, one clearly broken, falling down into a deep and frightening ravine below.

Desperately trying to adjust his own flying, he mentally reached out to see if he could pick up something from the hapless flier he had just grounded.

There was nothing. Maybe the other eMan was unconscious.

The last thing Zoarch saw was a few trees on the mountain side making uncanny movements as the derelict flier tumbled into the ravine and disappeared out of sight.

Zoarch was shaken down to his claws. He took one look at the ravine and realized that this was something completely different from the assisted takeoff at start rod.

Considering his present flying skills, he knew that if he landed there it would be hard for him to get airborne again. What had really happened? Was it his fault? The other guy should have seen it coming, right?

In the end he decided to call it a day.

Luckily he did not meet anyone before depositing his jet black wings in a rented basement locker. Knowing that his thoughts alone could give him away, he tried hard not to think of anything at all. Every time the unfortunate flight appeared in his mind, he hurriedly thought of something very pornographic in a desperate attempt to block it out.

He hurried out of Terminal 27.

Even though paranoia haunted him, Zoarch made it back home to his hotel without any problems. Although it was still early afternoon, he immediately got out of his walkers, made his night perch and fell asleep.

He woke up again as the light of day was fading.

In the vain hope of distracting his mind from unpleasant thoughts the turned on the teleNews.

But after a few minutes the speaker looked straight into the camera and said:

- Today the youngest member of the royal avian household, princess Saraya, disappeared while pleasure flying. A search has been underway for several hours, but her whereabouts are still unknown.

In his state of guilty paranoia, Zoarch felt that the speaker was looking straight into his eyes, providing this damning piece of information for him only. Even though he knew that the hotel room was supposed to be properly shielded from unwanted mental transactions, he hurriedly blocked the thought of golden wings falling into a ravine with a truly inappropriate picture of his own.

Just in case ...

Deep inside he felt an unsettling turmoil, a sea of desperation. If all of this really was his fault, he was doomed. If he was the one who had downed young Saraya, it would eventually be found out. He arrived at the inescapable conclusion that he had to do something about it.

In the lobby the clerk behind the counter greeted him on his way out.

It did not take long before he was standing on top of terminal 27, wings spread out wide, both claws firmly clenched on start rod.

This time things did not look so promising. It was pitch dark and the temperature had dropped considerably. On the up side, his feathers were charged to the max. Also, he had brought the night goggles that came with his space uniform.

Without much difficulty he made it back to the mountain above which the fatal collision had taken place. But he had to make several rounds before he could finally see the dreaded ravine through the night goggles.

Miraculously he made a perfect landing. But then came the hard part. Standing on the ground, in the darkness, he realized that the ravine was huge, a big gaping crack in the bedrock.

But there was only one thing he could do. He started searching.

He worked his way forward, staggering through uneven ground and heavy foliage, until his eyes finally caught a reflection. What he had found was half a golden wing. This made his heart jump, because it clearly indicated that the person he was looking for could not be too far away. He slowly made his way forward, away from the broken wing and deeper into the ravine.

It wasn't long before his avian senses told him that not so far ahead something was moving.

Her royal highness, princess Saraya, was lying on the ground, moaning. She was obviously in pain. Not only was her right wing broken, her right arm was broken too.

Zoarch sat down next to her. Disregarding the cold he took off the top part of his dress and used it as a primitive sling to steady her injured arm. When he was almost finished she finally opened her eyes.

- Who are you?
- Zoarch, he answered.
- Can you get us out of here?
- I will try.

He praised his good luck that it was a young female. If his victim had been a fully grown male, he would never have made it out of there. He lifted the young princess up and held her with both arms, her good arm across his shoulder.

Zoarch did his best to become airborne, but he needed four tries before he finally made it. After his second try she looked at him.

- You're not very good at this, are you?
- No, he said. Bear with me.

But soon enough they were flying. Slowly, and not very elegant, but they were flying.

From far away Zoarch could see Terminal 27 where all the lights were on. As soon as he landed, he was surrounded by uniformed eMen. The avian princess was being whisked away, but she still managed to turn around and look at him.

- Thank you, he heard her say.

Men in uniforms gave Zoarch a hard time. In the interrogation room he calmly told them the truth about everything that had happened from the moment he first took off at start rod until he finally made it back with the princess. Several of the policemen in the room were psychics, so there was no doubt about the veracity of his story.

In the end there was a knock on the door. A piece of paper made its way to the table in front of the police officer in charge. There was a brief consultation and then the officer who was second in command looked at Zoarch.

- The royal household does not wish to pursue this matter any further. There will be no charges. You are free to go.

Next morning a messenger appeared at Zoarch's hotel door. He delivered a formal message. It was not in the standard psychic format. Just like the message the police had received the night before where it said to let him go, this was written on a piece of paper.

> *Dear Mr. Zoarch,*
>
> *Allow us to express our gratitude for safely bringing home our young daughter. But at the same time we also hope you realize that your course of action can only be described as reckless and irresponsible. We do not understand why you did not report the incident to the authorities as soon as it had occurred. That would surely have saved all of us a lot of grief and unnecessary activity.*
>
> *Anyway, we – and most of all our daughter – want to thank you for the better part of the things you did. We understand that you are not an experienced flyMan and we also acknowledge that it must have taken quite a bit of courage to go searching for our daughter alone, in the wilderness, and in the dead of night.*
>
> *Tomorrow at noon there will be a modest reception at the sunSpot. We would like to see you there. If you bring this letter it will serve as your invitation.*
>
> *ZachaRita II, regna*

After reading this message, Zoarch did his best to keep his mind clear. By now he no longer had any faith whatsoever in the mental shielding of this particular hotel room. Or any other room for that matter.

He spent the rest of the day seeing sights and buying souvenirs.

Next morning Zoarch did not know how he was supposed to arrive at the sunSpot palace. He could, of course, fly. But would that be considered appropriate? And upon arrival what would he do with his wings? Consulting the terminal in his room, he could see that there was an inexpensive eTrain going straight to the sunSpot, so he decided to leave his wings at home and take the eTrain instead.

Before long he was sitting comfortably on a well polished rod in the eTrain passenger compartment. Next to him was a pretty young eGirl and what appeared to be her younger brother. The eBoy was not yet fully grown and seeing his eyes, Zoarch immediately knew that the boy was blind.

- *I hope it doesn't bother you*, the boy said without moving his lips.

Zoarch almost had a heart attack. He was still not used to the presence of so many psychics.

- *Don't worry*, the boy went on. *I won't bite you.*

- I sure hope not, Zoarch said out loud

The boy's sister who was sitting right next to the boy gave Zoarch a sharp look and then turned her attention to the brother.

- I told you not to contact people so freely. It is not polite.

The boy seemed to cringe a little under her rebuke. But it did not silence him completely.

- *Man*, the boy said while gently nudging his sister's side with an elbow. *Man, what a fine spaceship he's got.*

- What? The sister gave the boy another harsh look.

- *What kind a talk is this*, she said.

- I don't know, Zoarch said out loud. Leave me out of it.

- *Oh, you are such a liar*, the boy said with a big smile on his blind face.

- So, Sis, tell him about me, will you?

The girl sighed and shook her head. Most certainly the boy could not see it, but he seemed to know everything that was going on around him. The girl remained silent.

- You see, because I'm blind, my psychic abilities are extremely fine tuned, maybe because I need them so much. I can only see what I see through the eyes of other people, so therefore I have to be very good at it.

- No, no, no - you're not going to do any of your little parlor tricks in here. Her voice sounded downright threatening.

Zoarch felt that he had to do something.

- Maybe your brother sees the spaceship that brought me here. That was one big spaceship. Zoarch smiled affably at the boy who could not see him.

The boy blinked at him with his right blind eye.

- Yeah, yeah, was all that he said.

The train stopped at several stations, picking up passengers.

Between two stations Zoarch saw a huge billboard showing the well-known picture of Saint Flavian. The famous man flashed his usual paternal smile. On his right shoulder was the golden fowl, the bird that – according to legend – had provided mankind with the avian brain. Near the top of the billboard glowing letters spelled out - "The Man Who Changed Our World Forever."

Below the saintly picture, Zoarch managed to see the words "Saint Flavian's Day."

Now, at least he knew why the royals were having a party.

Soon after they arrived at the sunSpot.

The entrance to the royal castle was guarded by a huge eMan. The guard did not have his wings on, but he sure was heavily armed. He wore a black and blue dress that covered his entire body. On his chest, the royal crest was boldly on display.

Zoarch showed him the letter. The guard made no attempt of reading it, he just nodded. Zoarch went in.

The layout of the sunSpot appeared to be simplicity itself. A number of pavilions surrounded a circular open plaza. The weather was perfect. All the guests were mingling and talking in the open space and waiters in black and blue uniforms were serving drinks and snacks.

Zoarch felt more than a little lost. He did not know a single soul and he was definitely not a well-trained partygoer. Moving through the crowd he noticed that some of the guests wore golden masks. Were they trying to conceal their identity? Zoarch did not know.

A waiter handed him a glass of something bubbly. He tasted it and decided it was good. Trying to be discrete, he slowly made his way through the crowd. Suddenly a small person with a golden mask was blocking his way.

- How are you, she said.

- I'm good, but I don't quite know what to do.

- Well, at least try not to bump into anyone.

He gave her another look.

- It is you, isn't it. How is the arm?

- The arm is OK, it's my heart that is aflutter …

- I bet you say that to every passing bird.

Luckily for him she laughed. He could only see her mouth, but it looked like a smile.

- No ... and then again, yes. Some birds deserve special treatment.

She smiled again.

- Come meet my folks.

The royal couple was nice and polite. Zoarch thought that it must have been the queen herself who had sent the letter and during their conversation she seemed a bit more frigid than her husband, who was all smiles.

During the interview, Zoarch, sitting next to Saraya, were desperately broadcasting pictures of a broken golden wing in the faint hope of blocking peeping psychics.

Soon, however, the royal couple moved on to attend to other pressing duties.

Saraya looked at him quizzingly. It is hard to judge a person's intentions when you can only see their eyes and mouth. The golden mask covered the rest of her face. He still could not pick up on anything coming out of her mentally.

- Are you the adventurous type, she asked.

In light of everything that had happened, Zoarch had to agree.

- Then come, she said. There is something I would like to show you.

She led him down long corridors and stairs. It did not take long before he realized that they had left the modern part of the sunSpot and were heading into a much older part of the royal dwellings.

- One of the benefits of being a royal is that we have in our possession certain things that are not well known to the public and quite irreplaceable. Also – she looked him straight into the eyes – we would like to keep it that way.

- Have no fear, he answered. I am very good with secrets.

For a split second he thought that he heard her laugh.

- No, but really. What I am about to show you is not general knowledge.

She went on.

- I am sure that you know the official story. How original Earth itself became more and more polluted and hostile to man. How original man had trouble in space, mainly due to his body being very susceptible to hard radiation, gravitation and temperature fluctuations.

- So Saint Flavian produced the eMen, the hybrid supermen. Covered in a protective plumage of metallic feathers and strengthened mentally and physically by the inclusion of the avian brain, the eMen have now conquered the known universe.

She looked up to him, as if right now she was admiring the said conqueror.

- But what they do not tell you is that this did not happen all at one time. There was a lot of work, a lot of experiments that went well - and some that went not so well. It is a god thing to be part of a successful experiment. But it is not so great to be a failed, intermediate step along the way ...

- You can hardly be described as a failure, he said. You must be talking about somebody else, who actually became the victims of this process ...

- You are completely right, she said. My family, and a lot of other people were the ones who did much of the original experimental work. As a matter of fact, we feel rather guilty about certain things that happened back then. But on the other hand we have in our possession certain artifacts that were used in the process. One of these items I am about to show you ... now.

She put her hand on a bioReader and a door opened where only seconds before nothing but solid wall could be seen. She turned and looked at him.

- Some things have the power to change the course of your life, she said. If you are not ready, please say so now and we will go back to the party.

- I want to see your thing, was all that he said.

On the other side of the door Zoarch saw an apartment. To get into this apartment, however, you had to walk a short distance and cross what looked like a yellow screen (some sort of force field, Zoarch guessed). Inside the room, he could see furniture. But he failed to understand why the furniture looked so odd. Was it the yellow screen or ...

The princess took him by the hand and let him in. Silently, the door shut behind them. They were standing one step away from the yellow force field.

- Please take off your clothes and any wearables, she said.

Zoarch blinked.

Saraya had already taken off the few pieces of clothing and jewelry she was wearing. For the first time he could clearly see her naked black face. Zoarch stepped out of his walkers, took off what little clothes he was wearing and placed it on the floor, neatly folded, his eWallet on top.

Then she took him by the hand and together they stepped through the yellow delimiter.

Because he had never done it before, Zoarch stepped rather quickly into the room. Because of his hasty movements, the transformation took place even faster than it normally would have. Looking down on his right arm, Zoarch did not see a single feather. Also his skin was no longer black, but of a much lighter complexion. He ran his left hand up and down his right arm, and the skin was perfectly smooth. He looked further down and the rest of his body was the same.

Saraya opened a tall door. On the inside was a mirror. In the mirror he saw himself as a naked human male. To him it seemed like a small, but important relief that at least his hair was still black. Looking further down, he became aware of the raw nakedness of his sex. Looking up again, he saw Saraya.

This version of Saraya was not quite as tall as the one he was used to. Her hair was so fair that it hardly had any color at all. She beamed a smile at him.

- Welcome to the human world, she said.

Zoarch was stunned. He could not say a single word.

While Zoarch was looking down at his feet in bewildered disbelief, the royal princess gave him a push that landed him on an oblong piece of furniture, which turned out to be quite soft and rather comfortable. She then placed herself on top of him.

The eMan turned human did not know how to describe the things she did next, but it sure wasn't unpleasant.

In the end they both relaxed.

- What is this thing? What is it good for?

- It's a tool from back when they made the eMen. They needed something that could demonstrate the changing of genetics in real time.

- I never knew that any such thing was possible, he said. Why do you keep it a secret?

- The fear of a racial conflict is the main driver, she said. And even if they all knew about it and approved of it, maybe even wanted to use it, there are far too many eMen and only one place like this.

- And when we get out of here, we will be just like before?

- Yes, she said. Except now you know something that you did not know before you came here.

**Back at the modern SunSpot**, His Royal Highness, the King of EarthenScape, approached Zoarch.

- I hear my unruly daughter showed you the family heirlooms, he said with a big smile.

- She sure did.

- I have but two things on my mind, the king said. One is to live a peaceful life together with my friends and neighbors. The other is to make my daughter happy.

- Noble intentions, both of them, Zoarch remarked without sarcasm.

- A little while ago I heard a rumor that there would be some kind of inspection. Maybe somebody out there – he made an upwards gesture – did not believe that we truly follow the righteous path of all eMen here on EarthenScape. So I have been waiting for the inspector to arrive.

- And there you are, Commander. I hope you will enjoy your stay.

The king smiled, turned around and made himself scarce.

Zoarch was still reeling from the chock of hearing his military rank said out loud. He did notice, however, a not so tall figure which gently grabbed him by the arm.

- That is my father for you, she said. Such a nasty old bird. And here I am. His only daughter. Before somebody tells you in so many words or you figure it out yourself, I guess I will have to come clean. When I bumped into you, the only thing that was accidental was when my wing broke. I hadn't counted on that ...

- And here I thought that you actually liked me. He smiled.

- But I do, Commander. I really do.

This time his mind played a trick on him. When she smiled, he saw her human face instead of her black eMan features. It made him shiver. All his feathers tingled.

- Are there other things I need to see in order to fulfill my duties?

- I guess I haven't shown you anything but the most important stuff.

Very briefly he felt the touch of her body against his.

- I am impressed, he said. When my duties here are complete, maybe I will be able to see you again?

- But Commander, she said with a smile. Please don't wait too long ...

**Zoarch wanted to spend** his last day on EarthenScape in a way that was neither clandestine nor in the line of duty.

So he went to see Saint Flavian's Museum.

Outside the imposing building was a huge statue of Flavian himself. Being the one who 'fathered' the eMen, Saint Flavian was always depicted as a human. This was in fact the only human effigy allowed under eMan law.

Inside the museum was not so impressive. Apparently the big man had not left much behind to please the eyes of his devoted followers. A pair of gloves (much too small for any eMan) was the only real item said to belong to the Saintliness himself. The rest of the collection seemed more like a never ending praise of the eMen.

Zoarch had heard and seen all of this before, but nevertheless he now stopped in front of the info bots to see if he was missing something.

"During the lifetime of Saint Flavian, he worked diligently towards his big dream: the improvement of man himself. How can you improve on a being that has already conquered the world.

Saint Flavian knew that if man was going to conquer the great universe, he would have to change. Man would not be able to survive in space for prolonged periods of time. Flavian provided outstanding solutions to several problems. He heightened the intelligence of mankind by introducing new brain organs, already common in birds. He then improved and re-arranged the epidermis by introducing a layer of semi autonomous feathers, mainly controlled by the avian (bird) brain.

On the cellular level he came up with solutions to the telomeres, dramatically reducing the unnecessary aging process.

In a stroke of sheer genius, he modified reproduction to the laying of eggs. These eggs are easily controlled before hatching.

Also the timing of the hatching itself can be manipulated by various means and postponed for very long periods of time.

Having seen that all these things were good, Saint Flavian decided to leave the eMan realm. In order to prevent reactionary forces from undoing his improvements, he dismantled a major part of the tools he had used in the creation process and left EarthenScape in his private spaceship for a destination unknown.

Saint Flavian, we miss you and we honor your memory forever and ever."

Zoarch decided to call it a day. Soon he was back at the hotel, sleeping soundly, perched on his rod.

# Aftermath

Zoarch knew that the debriefing was going to be unpleasant. But it was even worse than he had anticipated. On the other side of the metal table he faced his boss, the Rear Admiral Zantos, and behind him three eMen with their BeakHelmets on. Zoarch knew that even though he could not see their faces, they could read his mind.

He told them every little thing. The color of his new wings. The wonderful flight. The horrific crash. The princess. The sunSpot. The room. The color of her human eyes. And – finally – what the King of EarthenScape had said to him.

The three faceless eMen never spoke a single word. But the Rear Admiral had lots of questions. Most of them were about the same thing. How did it feel to be human? He asked about the various body parts – starting with the head and moving down to the human foot – was it comfortable to walk around like that? Without claws? When the princess sat on top of Zoarch, how did that make him feel? And why did he mention the color of her eyes?

There were lots of questions. Zoarch answered all of them to the best of his ability – and all the while he tried not to think at all.

Finally it was over. The psychics left the room.

- You have done well.

The Rear Admiral looked him straight in the eyes.

- I hope you understand what this is all about?

- It is about the unity of the eMen.

- Yes. The unity of the eMen must not be disrupted by rumours about how good it is to be human. The mere thought that you can in fact become human again flies in the face of all the good things we have achieved. It has the potential to become a distraction of epic proportions. Only the top brass knows about this. They all agree that we need to be careful. Very careful, indeed.

- What about them? Zoarch nodded towards the door through which the three psychics had left the room.

- They will fill in their report and then their memories will be … redacted.

Zoarch could not get his head around the words he had just heard. The Rear Admiral seemed to read his mind.

- Yes, unfortunately. This is another thing that we would rather not talk about, but there is a well-established procedure. After the job is done they will not be able to remember what was said in here. But don't you worry. They are professionals. In their contracts it is stipulated that this is how things are done and they are compensated accordingly.

- Oh.

Zoarch was not sure what to believe.

- What about me, he finally asked.

- Don't you worry, Commander. You will be given a very attractive assignment that will bring you glory and, most likely, a promotion. In a few days you will be leaving for the Aidon Quadrant where our troops are struggling to avoid defeat. Your super heavy cruiser – and the 24 destroyers and 12 troop transporters that accompany you – will turn the tide.

Leaving the room, Zoarch realized that he had already been given a substantial promotion. On paper his rank remained the same, but he was now in charge of 37 intergalactic warships. Thousands of eMen were under his command - and he was tasked with winning a war.

# Are Four Legs Really Better Than Two?

*What do we know about the events that lead to her being crowned as the undisputed ruler, the Princess of the Forest? Not nearly as much as we would like to know, I can tell you that. Torin was – and it most certainly still is – a big place. If you venture deep inside the middle forest, no one will blame you for believing that the forest will continue and the trees will just go on and on forever. Deep inside that forest, the things we wish to know about the most are out of our reach and out of our sight, buried among dead leaves and the faded flowers of yesteryear.*

**I can show you** how my daughter looked when she finally came back home, passing through the green door and thus returning to the human world - if only for a little while. But that is only because Wendy (who happened to be there) made the famous painting. Shortly after the actual homecoming there was a brief session where Wendy made rough sketches and asked everybody to provide intimate details. In the painting we see Annabelle standing there, for the first time in years putting her clothes back on. We see my wife heading for the kitchen, still carrying the dirty water that she has just used to clean Annabelle after removing a lot of gritty and smelly forest stuff.

Along one wall we see a pair of jet black wings on the floor.

I also have in my possession the first hand written note made by Varna, describing the moment when for the first time our princess of the forest became aware of worlds outside of her own:

*"One day, late in the afternoon, Annabelle came running down the long, dark hills that separate Lonjo from Devashine. Passing the Badger Stream she noticed unfamiliar sounds coming from above. Looking up she saw something vaguely resembling fireworks in the sky. But unlike normal fireworks, this seemed to be coming down, instead of going up. Clearly, something was going on in the upper atmosphere, but Annabelle could not make any sense of it. Minutes later, all kinds of things were falling out of the sky and crashing down all around her".*

In the midst of this chaos Annabelle saw a figure falling to the ground. It looked human. Using her canine eyesight, which was not particularly well suited for this purpose, she realized that the unknown humanoid shape was coming down way too fast. In a desperate attempt to save the falling stranger from certain death, she ran as fast as she could towards the place of impact. She managed to get there only a split second before the stranger hit the ground. With all of her strength she hurled herself at the unknown person in order to break the fall and reduce the impact.

Less than three feet above the ground they crashed. Annabella was knocked out completely and lay still.

When she regained consciousness, her head was in the lap of the stranger. He gently stroked her ears and uttered soothing noises she did not understand. As his arm gently moved, all the black feathers tingled reassuringly.

- Great Torin, she thought. It's an eMan!

Seeing that her eyes were now wide open, the stranger let go of her.

- Thank you, he said. If not for you, I surely would have died!

Annabelle noticed that even though she clearly heard the spoken words, his lips never moved. That was even more scary. He was an eMan and a psychic too ...

Annabelle knew that she had to get away from him. Or else he would be able to take a good look inside of her mind. If someone like him were to acquire her intimate knowledge of the Torin rituals and practices, he could take everything for himself and she would not be able to stop him. She had to get away from this intruder and only one idea presented itself.

*She could go home.*

By chance she was very close to her family home, a place she had not visited for quite some time. But now, on the spur of the moment, she decided to run up to the house and jump straight through the green door. Once there, on the other side, she would stop. If he followed her through the active door, his innards would be turned inside out and he would die a horrible death. In case he did not follow her, she would be safe. In her human form he would never be able to access or manipulate her mind that freely and she could count on her family to vigorously defend the house.

So now she was running like the wind. And let us not forget that she was one with the forest and that all the trees and bushes of the middle forest truly loved her and helped her in any way. A big eMan with his wings on would not be able to follow her through the dense vegetation.

Having started, she concentrated on running as fast as she possibly could. Before long her canine nose started telling her a familiar story. She was home, back where it all started. Soon she could see the house and the green door right in front of her. She passed through the door, instantly, like a charged particle passing from anode to cathode.

All of her senses were screaming out loud that the menacing blackbird was right behind her. Having passed the green door, she took one more step inside the house. Then she turned around, ready to face whatever would come.

The active door sort of blitzed and for a split-second Annabelle couldn't see a thing. When her vision returned, she saw a naked man on the floor, coughing and spitting, holding a pair of jet black wings tucked under his left arm.

Zoarch looked at the naked girl standing before him. He did his best to regain his manly composure amidst the chaos he felt inside – also considering the fact that they were both naked and out of breath.

- What are you, Annabelle finally asked. Her voice seemed very small.

- I am Zoarch, he said, still coughing. Thank you for saving me.

At that moment a door burst open and people rushed in. Zoarch, in his human form, felt rather unsteady, so he just sat down on the floor and looked up at the girl.

It is not every day you see a wonder. But that day Zoarch could hardly get his eyes off young Annabelle. She was very beautiful.

And she was the spitting image of Princess Saraya of EarthenScape.

# The Insider

The big man looked at Zoarch.

- So you are a blueprint, he said.

It wasn't a question.

- There is a name for everything, or so they say. I think of myself as an ordinary person.

- Yes, of course. But an ordinary person would have been killed trying to get through the active door. So clearly, you are not ordinary – at all.

- Your daughter went through it, same as I did.

- And, unfortunately, there is no way she can be described as normal. Actually, we owe you something. You are the reason she finally had to come home. We haven't seen her in eight full years - and you are the one who made it happen.

The big man smiled.

- And still you tell me that you are just an ordinary fellow? Who are you, really?

- Zoarch.

- Do you have a rank?

- Commander.

- Again, not so ordinary. What do you command, a Destroyer?

- No ...

- Don't tell me you are in charge of a Cruiser.

- No ...

- Then what?

- A Dreadnaught.

- A Dreadnaught? What do you mean? I've never heard of any such thing.

- Actually, there is only one ... it's called The Lightspeed.

- And where is this so-called Dreadnaught of yours?

Zoarch pointed upwards.

- Right now you can't see it with the naked eye. Unless we make a real landing, the Lightspeed cannot go any lower than 1,500 feet. When we arrived, we first had to take out the planetary defenses. When we finally got down to 1,500 feet, I was way too optimistic. I just put on my wings and jumped. Unfortunately, I am not a very good flyMan and the conditions for flying weren't as good as I had hoped for. So instead of flying gracefully down to the surface, I fell like a stone. Luckily for me, that young lady of yours saved me.

- So you are telling me that you are the Commander of thousands of eMen?

- I don't like the sound of it, myself. But yes, I am the highest ranking eMan in this Galaxy.

For a brief moment the big man fell silent.

- My name is Borea, he said. Phillip Borea.

- You have already met my daughter. In her canine form, she is something like the ruler of this planet. They call her the Queen of the Forest. Welcome to our humble house.

- The pleasure is all mine, said the eMan momentarily turned human. I would very much like to borrow your restroom for a little while, and perhaps some clothes ...

**Much later that same night** he talked for a long time with Annabelle and Philip Borea. Sitting in the big kitchen he told them about his visit to EarthenScape.

- And she really flew into you, Annabelle said. She giggled.

- What did she look like, she went on.

Philip Borea had been talking quite a lot, but right now he did not say a thing. To Zoarch it seemed like he was embarrassed.

- She was very pretty, Zoarch answered. And very kind to me.

- Oh, now I know what you're talking about. She secured a sample of your dna, isn't that right, Mr. Blueprint. The girl in front of him smiled, innocently.

Zoarch felt that the conversation was taking something of a turn.

- She also told me certain things about this galaxy.

Now he was deliberately trying to steer the conversation away from the obvious.

- So after having achieved our military objectives, I ordered a troop transporter and The Lightspeed to go to a certain planet called Rani.

When he heard the name Rani, Philip Borea blinked. But only once.

- There I had a very interesting conversation with an old man called Joshua. I asked for a certain thing called the editor, did he still have it? He said yes. He had it. But it needed certain other things to function properly, namely an active door – and a power source. He told me that both of these items could be found here on Torin, hidden by woods and mountains, and guarded by someone older than time.

- When we arrived here, we found the whole planet locked down by planetary defenses, Zoarch went on. I don't know who set it up, but I guess it wasn't you. Well, you know the rest. We took out the old-fashioned defense mechanisms and I jumped. And here we are.

- So what you have come here for is actually this power source, Annabelle inquired.

- Yes, that is my primary objective.

Philip Borea had something on his mind.

- These things you talk about were used to create the eMen. If you manage to put all of this stuff back together again, what will you do with it? Will you turn the eMen back into humans? Will you make a new and better generation of eMen? What is your plan?

- I don't know, Zoarch answered. I guess I will try to make our lives better. I will do whatever I can so that everybody can live better lives. Being an eMan isn't that bad. We are much stronger than ordinary human beings and the Avian brain helps us in so many ways that I can hardly count them all. But no one ever told me that it was possible to change back, to become human again - like I am right now.

As he spoke these words, he held his hands up in front of him. Even now he still expected to hear the familiar tingle of small black feathers moving. But there were no sounds and his skin - which ought to be pitch black - still had an odd, creamy color.

Through the open door to the living room something hurried in. It jumped straight into Philip Borea's lap. He started petting the animal, as if it was an old-fashioned cat.

Zoarch looked at the animal. He had never seen anything like it, so he figured it must be indigenous to Torin.

Philip Borea noticed his interest.

- It's a Prollock, he said. There aren't many of them, these days. The way I remember it there used to be more of them.

- Don't worry, he added. He pushed back the creature's lips. Zoarch saw a mouth full of big teeth.

- So long as they don't go bad they are strictly herbivores. We feed it leaves from outside and kitchen waste.

- What happens when they go bad?
- Bad Prollocks are really dangerous. They get bigger. Their teeth also become bigger and they start eating flesh ...

**Two days later** they set out for the mountains in the North.

Annabelle went out through the green door and Zoarch exited through a regular door. Standing outside, he was still a man while she was now in her canine form.

The night before that they had come to a decision.

- Will you go with me to the power source? I have to find it and it would be so much easier if you would come along.
- I am not sure that I understand what my role will be, she answered. But, yes. I am coming with you. It is my duty to oversee all unusual events – on behalf of Torin, of course.
- How will we get there? Should I go as a man or as an eMan?
- I would very much prefer it if you stay the way you are right now. I am not quite comfortable with eMen.
- If I go as a man, you will have to wait for me. As a man, I feel rather feeble. This body is not fit for hiking through a forest.
- Don't worry. You are with me. You'll be fine.
- If you say so.

Outside the air was cool and crisp. Sun beamed through the treetops like tiny rivers of molten gold.

With regard to clothes, Annabelle's family had quickly copied the design of his flyMan outfit – black with red trimmings – and he was now wearing their homemade creation. The fact that he did not have any shoes, however, was downright disturbing. How could he traverse a huge forest barefoot?

It seemed like this time around, Annabelle were the one who could read his thoughts.

- Don't worry too much about it, she said. Let's get going.

Taking his first human steps on Torin, he soon found out what she meant. Together with Annabelle he was wearing the whole forest like a protective cover.

The forest obeyed her to an astonishing degree – and being with her, Zoarch received an unprecedented level of service.

Whenever he took a step, his foot would find an abundance of green lush mosses, so soft to step on that it seemed like he was walking on a huge, super soft carpet. Bushes and branches would move out of his way, as if guided by invisible hands.

Moving forward, deeper into the middle forest of Torin, the feeling of being one with all this living matter struck a deep chord inside of him. He realized that this forest would never become the realm of neither man nor eMan. The fact that he could be here at all was due to a beautiful girl who walked right there in front of him in the shape of a wolf.

They came to the Badger Stream.

For a few brief moments the water stopped running and the stream went silent. Earth gathered on both banks, until it almost formed a small bridge. Effortlessly, they jumped from one side to the other. Crossing the stream this way was child's play.

When the stars came out, Annabelle did not stop. Zoarch followed right behind her.

- Where are we going?

- We are going to the Torin palace.

- What is that?

- It is my other 'home'.

- Oh.

He could still hear her inner voice, but in the shape of man he was unable to penetrate her deeper thoughts.

That did not stop him, however.

- What is the Torin palace like.

- You will see. You have arrived at a fortunate moment in time. Tomorrow it is rejuveNight and we will celebrate the annual rejuvenation ceremony.

- It sounds like a big thing.

- It is. Just about everbody will be there. Except for the bad Prollocks, of course.

- The bad Prollocks?

- Just a bad joke of mine. Most likely you will never see one ...

- Then what will I see?

- You will see all the members of the deer tribe, you will see all the members of the badger clan and my tribe, the wolf clan.

- Will the wolves eat the deer?

- No, basically we are all herbivores and we don't eat all that much in the first place.

Her inner voice sounded amused, as if he had said something funny.

- How about this thing I am looking for, the power supply. When can we start searching for it?

- When the rejuvenation ceremony is done, I will have to rest for a while. When I wake up again, we will start looking for it.

- Good!

They continued their march through the forest until the last light of day faded. Annabelle picked out a suitable spot and they sat down. Immediately twigs and leaves piled up behind Zoarch's back. He allowed himself the luxury of sinking into it. More leaves settled on top of him. When the light of the second moon gently touched his face, Zoarch closed his eyes for just a little while. It had been a long day.

The tired Commander slept like a baby.

Annabelle looked at him. They were perfectly safe. More than 10 hours ago her entire tribe had caught up with them. The wolf clan were all around her, she could smell them, she could feel their presence.

**Deep inside the middle forest**, Zoarch woke up to a new day of adventure.

His breakfast was laid out next to his 'bed' and consisted of roots and beets. There was a small water stream nearby and he went there to wash the soil off his breakfast.

Half an hour later they were walking. None of them talked very much. Zoarch had expected her to have questions about life on other planets, but she never asked. He had a lingering feeling that he ought to ask her about the ways and customs of her peers, but somehow he felt embarrassed and never got to ask the right questions. He guessed that she probably felt the same way.

Hours later, past midday, they encountered higher grounds. Soon he realized that they were slowly, but surely heading for the highest mountaintop.

But he still had no trouble walking leisurely ahead and even jumping over small obstacles felt easier than it should have been.

Up and up they went.

At last they came to where the tree line ended. Zoarch could see that they were standing on the outskirts of a flat, grassy plain. Right in the middle of the big plain there was an elevated object that he could not account for.

- What is that thing, he asked and pointed to it.

- This, she said, is the Torin palace. A little further up the mountains there are caves, quite pleasant ones if I may say .The thing you asked about is the center of our world, our altar so to speak. In a few hours we will all witness the ceremony together and then you will see for yourself what this is all about.

He felt a burning desire to see her in the shape of a woman again. It was rather unnerving having to hear all this from a wolf, but then again ... maybe she wished for him to become a wolf too?

While they moved across the huge lawn, the entire wolf clan came out in the open like a big wave of animals. Soon the canines walked in straight lines on both sides of them. Zoarch tried to count the members of the wolf tribe. In the end he gave up and concluded that there were at least one hundred.

Annabelle was heading for the caves. So once again they went up. The caves were a marvel – spacious, clean and dry. Right outside the entrance there was a small waterfall. From their present vantage point, they could see all of the grassy area with the so-called altar standing prominently in the middle.

Down below, more tribes were arriving. For some reason the deer tribe had not arrived yet. Looking down, he could see that something - or someone - was slowly, but steadily coming towards them. When the bent figure came nearer, Zoarch could see that it was a Prollock.

Annabelle ran down to meet it. Zoarch realized that there was some kind of psychic conversation going on between the two of them, but he did not understand anything of what was actually being said.

Annabelle returned to his side.

- A member of the deer tribe has been killed. It is my duty to inspect the crime scene.

- Well, let's do it.

They walked through the trees for about ten minutes before arriving at a small clearing. The carcass was there, so there was no doubt about them being in the right place. The deer had been ripped open. It was a ghastly sight.

Zoarch was a professional soldier. He had seen worse than this. Annabelle, on the other hand, seemed to be emotionally disturbed by the bloody remains.

Rather than concentrating on the victim, Zoarch searched the surroundings. Soon he found large tracks leading away, to the North.

He called Annabelle. Again, he wished for her to be human so that he could understand her bodily expressions and react accordingly. He had no previous knowledge of canines; when it came to the behavior of four-legged beings, he was a poor judge.

- I am worried, she said. I believe that this is indeed the work of a bad Prollock, the very thing I joked about earlier. Also, one more member of the deer tribe is missing.

- We must leave the corpse here and return. We cannot be late for the ritual.

Not much was said on their way back to her palace.

**The day was ending**. It seemed to Zoarch that this day had passed much more quickly than the previous one.

Looking up, he could see that this was because only the lesser sol was out and now the smaller moon were climbing across the heaven above. From the looks of it, this moon would soon be right above them. It seemed appropriate, but hardly a coincidence.

By now the deer tribe had arrived and the plain below the palace were filled with animals. The small badgers formed the inner circle. After them came the wolves. The deer formed the outer ring.

Slowly but surely they started circling the altar clockwise.

The light from the lesser sol faded, but in the clear moonlight it was as if Zoarch could see a luminous energy that spread from the altar and out.

Where the uncanny light hit the animals, it appeared to him that they slightly changed. He could not, however, understand what he saw.

The animals were now giving off sounds. The grunts of the badgers, the howls of the wolves and the deer noises all mixed into a steady hum.

The living ring of tribal animals circled the altar, faster and faster.

At a certain point in time the last light of sol was gone and as the moon was now right above them, Zoarch could still see all the animals. None of them had a shadow.

There was a slight vibration coming from the ground below. Zoarch was taken by surprise as a piller of light rose from the altar and touched the moon above. This light made the moon change color from dull gray to shiny gold.

As if this marvel was not enough, a new light had descended on the circling animals. A golden shine lay over them as a floating curtain and round and round they went, faster than ever before. The bright light drew huge shadows of the circling animals on the surroundings.

He had been so obsessed with what was going on that he did not realize that Annabelle had left his side. Now he saw her running full speed just outside of the three animals rings. It went on for some time, faster and faster they were running, in the end it was as if he saw her only as a blur. It was as if she drew a fourth ring of her own, outside of the crowded center.

Then the pillar of light retreated. Once more the color of the moon changed to gray. All the animals stood still and howled.

The ritual was over.

Zoarch saw the badgers and the deer disappear into the woods. The wolves stayed with Annabelle and soon they all lay in the grass outside the caves.

Annabelle returned to his side. She was lying on her back, wriggling in the tall grass, all four legs in the air.

She seemed happy.

It had been a long day. Soon he was sleeping in the grass.

Next morning he woke up and found his usual breakfast waiting, roots and beets. He did not mind. By now he had clearly understood that this was not a carnivorous planet.

- We should be going soon, she said. I want to find this thing you are looking for. I need to get to the bottom of this, too.

- What about our friend, the bad Prollock.

- I have asked my tribe to search for it. They will let us know if they find it.

Soon after they were moving slowly towards higher ground.

The middle forest were now far behind them and they were making their way into the Northern mountains. On the outskirts of the forest, Zoarch had found some broad, very sturdy leaves. He tied several of these big leaves around his feet. It wasn't perfect, but for now it worked.

- Do you even know where we are going, he asked?

- I think so. Have patience.

When the light began to fade, he realized that they had not covered much ground. But on the other hand logic told him that the thing they searched for could not be too far away from the so-called palace.

- We are being hunted, she said.

- What?

- It's that Prollock. It is following us, right down there.

- What should we do?

- The place we are looking for is up ahead. Maybe when we are inside the cave, we can hide from the Prollock.

But events did not turn out in that way. They had to climb to reach the cave. When Zoarch finally made it to the entrance, the bad Prollock finally caught up with them. Seeing it for the first time, Zoarch was surprised just how much bigger it was than the Prollock he had seen back at the house. Its hide was ghostly white and it had an ugly big mouth full of teeth that glistened in the last light of day. Zoarch grabbed a big rock – he could hardly lift it in his fragile human form – and hurled it at the animal. He hit it and it did actually slow down. But it still kept on coming. Luckily its body was not well suited for mountain climbing.

Zoarch gave the wolfgirl a good shove that landed her at the tunnel entrance.

- Hold on to my tail, she said. If I fall down, then hold me.

Inside the cave turned into a pitch-black tunnel.

- Hold on now, Annabelle said.

Slowly she led him forward. Behind him he could still hear horrible Prollock noises.

Cautiously they moved forward in the darkness. This, however did not last long.

Suddenly there was a clicking sound and a blue door came alive right in front of them.

Without the slightest hesitation they jumped right through it. Inside they looked at each other. Annabelle was once again a human – and Zoarch was pleased to hear the familiar tingle of little black feathers.

Then the door blitzed and there was a terrible roar. When they were able see clearly again, the remains of the bad Prollock lay on the floor between them. It seemed smaller now. Visually it was out of shape. Things were not where they were supposed to be. As they watched, a final convulsion shook the poor beast.

Annabelle pointed to a pair of deer antlers sticking out of the creature's hairy chest.

- This is horrible, she said. This must be the second, missing member of the deer tribe. It killed and ate one of its own kind.

The dead body still gave off little whiffs of white smoke. Also they could smell the singed meat.

They got up. Annabelle was stark naked. Their eyes met.

- By now you must be used to seeing me like this?

Zoarch did not answer. Instead he turned around and walked further down the tunnel.

This part of the tunnel was sparsely lit. They moved slowly forward until they came to where the tunnel opened into a cavern. In the middle of the cavern were odd shapes that most of all looked like furniture. On a table lay something that looked like a silvery crown. Zoarch picked it up and jokingly he put it on.

The lights went on, big screens on the walls came alive, showing pictures of the entrance they had just passed, other rooms that they had never seen before. Two big screens were dedicated to the Torin palace. Another screen showed a schematic of the so-called altar.

- This must be the power source. I suspected it already yesterday when that big light touched the moon above.

She looked at him bewildered.

- But what is this, he said and pointed to a red dot at ground level.

- It is the red door, said an unfamiliar voice. There are four doors and this is the red one.

Another screen came alive and from there a solemn face looked down upon them. Clearly it was the face of Saint Flavian himself.

- Welcome, boomed the voice. I am the keeper of Master Flavians teachings. If you will be so kind as to listen to me for a moment, I have a few things to tell you.

They both stood still and said nothing.

- Sensor data tells me that there are two living persons in here. One ID signature I know already.

The other person must be a blueprint from outside of this world. Master Flavian always wished for someone to carry on his work. I will offer this task to you and help you as best as I can.

- Certain things may seem a bit shocking to you. Let me start with a brief history lesson.

- When Flavian explored what was left of a rogue planet that was drifting through space on its own - without any sun that is - he found an alien spaceship.

- From this ship he salvaged as much as he could – the items included the power supply, the four doors and the sad remains of an alien.

- Being a genius, he managed to 'read' parts of the alien brain. Realizing how it worked, he very soon arrived at the idea that some of its neural circuitry could be fused - or rather combined - with the human brain. He also realized that such an outcome would not be immediately acceptable to the human population at large, so he came up with the bird story, about the so-called avian brain, helping mankind to become stronger and to venture further out into the universe.

- He soon discovered that he could fuse neural circuits copied from the alien brain with human brain tissue by using the four doors. So he started out on a very small scale. There were many trials and errors and, unfortunately, many people died in the process.

- Master Flavian realized that the major problem arose from errors in the human genome. In order to bypass this hurdle he needed a blueprint – a perfect specimen, with which he could compare his test subjects and repair their dna accordingly.

- In his EarthenScape laboratory Master Flavian managed to produce two such blueprints – one male and one female.

- After that the official story is almost true. Master Flavian successfully introduced the eMan to the world. He then copied the dna of the persons he cared for the most and stored their vital information. Shortly after he took his leave of a world that was no longer human and flew here. His spaceship is parked in a cavern not far from here. It is out of fuel, but otherwise fully functioning.

The light on the screen flickered. For a moment the picture was garbled.

- From the data he had brought with him, the Master recreated his friends. But he found this planet to be a horrible, lonely place. Knowing that he would very soon reach the end of his own life, he worried about the mental health of those he left behind. This prompted him to re-create the female blueprint. He then used some obscure features of the power source to make the biggest forest of the planet 'come alive'. To this very day the whole forest is enveloped in a permanent force field that is controlled by the Master's final creation – she who is standing here before me – the copy of the female blueprint.

- The only local species of animals, the Prollocks, he changed into three earth-like creatures. Coming here, you must have seen them – the wolves, the badgers and the deers.

- Finishing these things, the Master felt the end approaching. The last thing he did before he died was to activate the old planetary defenses.

- Everything here belongs to the legacy of Saint Flavian. He did what he could, while he was still alive. Now it's your turn. Everything you need is here. If you need me, just call out for Servus.

The screen went blank.

- It looks like we have been given a job, she said.

- You are right. But luckily we have help.


**The shuttle with her family** arrived five hours later. It looked to Zoarch as if they had brought each and every item from the house, including the green door.

Philip Borea gave him the eye.

- Hello, Commander, what is the rush?

- I am sorry about that, Philip. But I guess it is necessary. Annabelle will be here any moment and she will fill you in.

Philip Borea turned his attention to the shuttle and then he smiled.

- So that is your spaceship, the so-called Dreadnaught?

- Not quite.

- Where is it then?

- In orbit. You just wait and see. We will use the shuttle to move all our stuff up to the Lightspeed.

Annabelle arrived.

- Hi dad.

- My darling.

- Hi Zoarch.

Zoarch wondered how smoothly things would go.

He remembered the words "not immediately acceptable to the population at large."

He would just have to be careful. Very careful.

Two hours later the Lightspeed's tech crew arrived on the other shuttle.

Their first task was to drill through the bedrock to make a new entrance to the cave laboratory. They were not blueprints, so they could not pass the blue door.

Once they were inside, Zoarch briefed their boss, a young eMan, lieutenant Zonos. Zonos was widely known as a whiz kid.

Zoarch pointed to a diagram showing the layout of the altar.

- You will have to be very careful with this one, he said. The output of this thing is beyond anything we can come up with ...

One third of the new arrivals went looking for Saint Flavian's spaceship.

As promised they found it to be in good shape and two shuttle trips were enough to refuel the famous vessel.

Later, Annabelle and Philip Borea came to see Zoarch.

Annabelle did not hold back.

- I understand that you are about to destroy our world?

- It will not be destroyed, but it will not remain the same. That is for sure.

Philip Borea held his pet Prollock in his arms.

- What about these guys, he asked. From what Annabelle tells me, I understand that all of the animal tribes are really Prollocks and when you cut the power supply, they will all go back to being Prollocks again. Will they be good or bad Prollocks?

- I haven't been through all of his papers. But Flavian clearly states that we have a choice. We can see to it that they all become nice little Prollocks again, like the one you are holding close to your heart. Or we can make them all bad. The thing is that by making them bad, we will create a short cut in their evolution which will probably save them millions of years.

- You and Annabelle gets to decide. This is your home. You decide what is best.

- What about us? The big man looked as if he was about to cry.

- You will get a free ride to EarthenScape on the most famous spaceship in the known universe. When we get there, we will set up the four doors and demonstrate to every living soul that a new paradigm has come to stay. You can bring your Prollock, it will be good for publicity ...

Zoarch noticed that Annabelle gave him a peculiar look, almost disapprovingly. For once, he did not know what to say.

**Back on EarthenScape** the shuttle landed on the lawn right next to the sunSpot palace.

Standing in front of the palace, the guards looked as if they were going to forbid him entrance, but before they could take any action, a slender eGirl emerged.

- What brings you here, Commander?

- I have serious business that I need to discuss with you and your father.

- So it will be all business and no fun?

- Oh, we will have fun. Believe me, this is going to be very entertaining.

Past the door, he felt her body against his. As they passed down the corridors all her little feathers seemed to be tingling with joy.

- Thank you for coming, the king beamed a welcoming smile at him. Now I may finally get to see a smile on my daughter's face again.

- Thank you very much.

In the King's office he laid out the results of his voyage.

- You say you have everything, except the dead body itself?

- Yes. There is, however, a few hickups as in severe Public Relation problems. I worry that the eMen will not take kindly to the news that the avian brain is in fact an alien brain. It must be presented in such a way that the pros clearly outnumber the cons.

- If what you say is true, we will be able to cure almost every disease and travel huge distances without discomfort or time lapses. That must count for something.

- Also I wonder what the SEC will have to say?

- Yes, the Superior eMan Council surely expects the rest of us to obey. Would they be able to stop your presentation with brute force.

- No, I don't think so. The eMen under my command are very loyal. They are well aware of what we have accomplished. The Lightspeed can take on any weapon system in space. We have already blown up more enemies than I care to think about.

But – more to the point – they handed me this mission because I am the blueprint. Not in spite of it.

- Is there anything you need?

- If we can use your facilities, especially the yellow door, then we can be ready by the day after tomorrow.

**Zoarch worried that** he could not present the new female blueprint to the eMen in her human form. So he had Annabelle flown in on the shuttle. Together they walked down the royal corridors behind a guard. When they came to the yellow door, the guard turned around and left them alone. Zoarch was just about to ask Annabelle to pass the active door when another human form appeared to the left of them.

- My, my, said the princess Saraya. Who is this lovely person?

Annabelle courtsied.

- I am an innocent young woman from the planet Torin. This horrible eMan has completely ruined my homeworld, following which he forcibly abducted me and brought me here.

- But why do you look exactly like me?

- Because that was what Saint Flavian had in mind when he made me.

- And what does the Commander intend to do with you now?

- He will ask you to bring me into this chamber by the back door, so that we can both go out through that yellow door I see over there. He says that will turn both you and I into adorable eGirls.

- Well, we better comply with his Lordship's wishes. Or else he may turn us into something awful.

The princess nodded to Zoarch.

- I have laid out some clothes in there, she said and nodded towards the chamber.

The girls hurriedly disappeared behind an ordinary door.

Zoarch went into the chamber through the yellow door and entered the room as a naked human male.

He put on the clothes that Saraya had prepared for him. While he was buttoning the shirt, he heard a small cough from behind.

There, in the farthest end of a sofa, sat a very small human boy.

Zoarch was rather surprised. He would never have thought that Saraya would bring children to this particular place.

The child looked up at him.

- Are you my father?

- I am Zoarch.

- And I am Zenith. Mama said she would be here soon.

Zoarch sat down on the sofa next to the kid. He arrived at the only logical conclusion. There could be no other explanation for the kid being in this particular room.

- Yes, he said and smiled reassuringly. I believe I am your father.

When the girls entered the room from behind the furniture, they saw little Zenith sitting on Zoarch's lap, his arms around him as if he would never let go.

**The presentation was a blast**. Before the day was over, more than 90% of all eMen had seen it.

Standing in front of his palace, the king himself introduced the sensational news.

- The SEC sent him to another galaxy on a double mission, the king said. One goal was to defeat the secession forces, thus securing the strength and unity of the eMen. Another objective was to find the remains of Saint Flavian.

(The on-screen image showed a small spaceship approaching EarthenScape).

- On the planet Torin his hard work was rewarded when he uncovered everything the Saint had left behind, except for Saint Flavian himself. It is said that his ashes are buried on Torin, in a secret place somewhere in the endless forests. But his ship was found to be intact and it only needed re-fueling to become fully operational. We now know that the Saint continued his work for several decades until at last he died of old age.

(Close-up of the spaceship, now slowly descending to the EarthenScape spaceport.)

- Like everybody else, Saint Flavian needed friends. On Torin he re-created some of his best friends from his former life. He also re-created a copy of the female blueprint and made her the regent of that planet.

- The SEC in its wisdom sent out our male blueprint to get the job done. Nobody else than our very own Commander Zoarch could have succeeded so well.

- It is his native ability to pass through the active doors that has led to the astounding results, of which you are about to learn.

A big crowd of eMen had now gathered around the landed spaceship. When the survivors from Torin appeared on the tarmac, spontaneous applause was heard. The last one to come out was the female blueprint and the sight of her made the crowd go wild.

- We will now present you with the miracles our Saint produced in his lonely exile.

- I hereby give the word to Commander Zoarch himself.

- **Dear friends. Today** will be a day to remember. What you are about to witness is nothing less than a paradigm shift. Occasionally, emerging technologies have the ability to transform society – even in unexpected ways. Throughout his long life, Saint Flavian was the driving force behind the making of the eMen. I am talking about the making of all of us. The benefits of the transition from human beings to eMen were great, but it also came with a high price. We changed - and in the process we got stronger. We changed - and therefore we were able to conquer space.

- But many aspects of life changed for the worse. The eMen does not give birth to living children. When the children are hatched, the state is there to care for them – while you and I are away, working for the common good, often far from home.

- The changes to the human genome were comprehensive. The first eMen had dna that actually worked, but it was too damaged to be replicated or transformed. Saint Flavian used an active door to facilitate the transformation from human beings to eMen. But the first eMen were too damaged to pass back again through the active door. In short, they had become eMen - but now they could not change back into their human form.

- The active doors are unable to successfully process any living being with less than 97.8% intact dna. If the percentage of damaged dna is higher, the door will let the subject in, but when it tries to rebuild that entity on the other side, the non-compliant dna will cause irreversible damage and the living being that it once was will come out on the other side, deformed and dead.

- One of the first things Saint Flavian did was to build a set of blueprints, one male and one female. The active doors were thus provided with a 100% correct reference from which it could – and still can – insert fully functioning strings of dna as needed. I don't know how many people died before the blueprints, of which I am one, were finalized. But it must have been many. Too many.

- All of the survivors from the Earth catastrophe were voluntarily turned into first generation eMen. A few months later the Hatchings began. So from this date and on we have all been proud eMen.

- I believe that Saint Flavian was unhappy with all the lives that were lost. So he kept working, trying to improve his methods with only one objective in mind, namely that we can all live better lives.

- The SEC, however, did not approve of his new line of experiments. They feared that the end result would be more dead eMen, and they firmly believed that it was for the best if all eMen and eWomen were the same kind of beings. If someone produced a new and better eMan, this might lead to trouble. That is how they reasoned.

- Therefore, they put pressure on Saint Flavian and told him to stop experimenting and also they told him to go away. I will return to this in a minute.

- The Saint packed up his belongings. It is said that he spread out his scientific machinery, hiding bits of it here and bits of it there. In fact he only left one thing behind. He left one active door on EarthenScape. The rest he jammed into his spaceship. Then he flew straight to Torin. Before he landed, he put a number of old fashioned armed satellites in orbit as a primitive planetary defense mechanism. He clearly wanted to be left alone.

- The Saint never meant to produce monsters. Having arrived on Torin, he reproduced his best friends and the female blueprint. He then turned the biggest forest on that dark planet into a magnificent magic landscape, where each and every little thing obeyed the wishes of the female blueprint.

- Now I will return to the reason why the SEC could force Flavian into exile. This is the part of the story you have never heard before. When Saint Flavian was very young he was in charge of a salvage vessel. One day, on some forsaken planet far away from here, he came across an alien spaceship - with a dead alien inside. Saint Flavian worked his salvage machinery like a madman. When he left that planet, he brought three things with him: a power supply, an active door and every bit of biological information he could squeeze out of the dead alien.

- What I am trying to tell you is that our avian brain does not come from some kind of extinct bird. It comes from a dead alien. The reason why you were kept in the dark is because the SEC did not think that the general public would be able to accept this knowledge.

- Today we are taking the work of Saint Flavian to the next level. First I will give you a demonstration of how active doors can be used. Then I will discuss the ramifications of this demonstration. Please have patience with me ...

Zoarch unveiled a graphic showing the power source and three active doors - blue, green and red.

He demonstrated that each door had its own properties, but also that they were programmable.

- Here we see two blue doors. We will use them to repair the dna of a first generation eMan. One side of the first blue door will read the eMan. Normally the other side of that same door will try to recombine him. But since that would be fatal, we have disabled this function and instead he is passed on to the second blue door. The front side of this door will compare the received output to a correct blueprint. The necessary changes will be implemented and the other side of that second door will then recombine him. If this procedure is implemented successfully, the eMan will now be a fully functioning blueprint.

- Already all eMen on the Lightspeed and the accompanying transporters have been through this procedure.

- Another feature of the active doors is instant transportation. From one active door you can jump to any other door, no matter where it is. This will greatly enhance our combat abilities and improve our chances to survive in case of life-threatening disasters. There may be a limit to how far you can go, but we have not reached that limit yet.

- You may ask yourself what else can be achieved by using these new tools. I can only give you one answer.

Please allow me to introduce her royal highness, the princess Saraya of EarthenScape, and my son Zenith.

Saraya walked down the aisle, holding Zenith's hand. Soon they were standing next to Zoarch. With the smiling eBoy sitting on his left arm, Zoarch held up his right hand and loudly exclaimed:

- *This is a new dawn for all eMen, praise the Saint.*

# On My Way to Sainthood

When the presentation was over, we quickly packed up our gear. Most of the science stuff went into the Saint's ship, which by now had become widely known as The Salvation. En route from Torin to Earthenscape we had already scanned and copied every little item from Torin. We could replicate gates and as long as it was a small number of gates we could operate them using only our standard power units. We also set up a red door on the Lightspeed and another red door on The Salvation.

Then we took apart the yellow door on Earthenscape and put it together again in another, hidden location. The plan was to show possible SEC inspectors the original, now abandoned room and the king would assure everybody that the yellow door was now flying through space on board The Salvation.

Also on board The Salvation were the inhabitants of Torin. Princess Saraya and little Zenith occupied the Commander's cabin on the Lightspeed.

**The control panel attached** to the blue door blinked. I bent over and pressed a button. The door blinked and in came Philip Borea.

The control room was rather cold. It was not cold enough to make an eMan uncomfortable, but Philip Borea was an elderly human being. I had asked the crew to find a jacket for him. When he tried it on, it turned out to be a perfect fit.

He looked briefly at his own reflection in a shiny metal panel next o the blue door. Then he smiled.

Zoarch's feathers tingled approvingly. Still holding the Master Joystick, he looked down on the scrawny human figure standing next to him.

- You are no doubt aware that spaceships such as the Lightspeed always has an Executive Officer on board to relieve the duties of the Commander, he said.

- I just met him.

- I know you did. This is what I would like to ask you. Ever since we left EarthenScape, my XO has been totally committed to steering The Salvation. Therefore I think it is about time that you pilot your own ship, so I can have him back.

Philip Borea looked like he was the one that had been taken back. Then he raised his eyes and looked Zoarch straight in the eyes.

- What gave me away?
- The red door on Torin.
- The red door?
- Yes, because when I finally learned about the existence of the red door right next to the power source, your cozy little set-up was easy to understand.
- I see. Philip Borea sighed.
- But it sure was convenient, he went on. No matter where I was, I could always get to the power source and fix whatever needed to be fixed.
- I am glad that we understand each other, Zoarch said – but this time without moving his lips.
- There is one more thing. The revised story we just presented to all of the known universe – that you found a dead alien and used his brain – is not quite accurate, is it? There was no dead alien. You used yourself and your own brain as a model, simple as that.
- There is no hiding anything from you, is there?
- Not if I can help it. Zoarch laughed.
- My original ship is still on Torin. I would very much like to fly The Salvation back to Torin and park it there. Then I will have some fun with setting up the enchanted forest one more time. After that I will carefully consider what to do next.
- What am I supposed to call you?
- It is for the best if you stick with Philip Borea. It will keep us out of trouble. One day I will tell you my real name …
- But actually there is one more thing I would like you do for me? The Saint smiled. I need you to come on board The Salvation and donate something of your own to my young blueprint. Same procedure as last time, if I may say so …

Apparently, you cannot keep a good Saint down.

It took Zoarch several minutes to come up with a suitable answer to that one.

# Life After Brenda

We did not speak until we were on the plane. Flying back to France made my mood a little better. But the image of Brenda was still troubling me.

- You must try to forget it, Becky told me. There is nothing you can do.

- But it is more than horrible. The way she looked ...

- Then you should have seen her on the inside. They have wired her like a goddamn explosive xmas tree. Even if I knew precisely what they did, I doubt that it can be undone.

- I feel so guilty about it.

- You are not. Those bastards who did this is to blame. When something like that is about to go down, you have a right to save yourself. If you had not tried to escape, you would quite simply be like her now. With another person or two inside of you.

I knew that he was right. But I also remembered that fateful night when Brenda tried to kill herself.

- So you say there is no way to save her.

- That is correct. Even if I re-wire her to not seeing her old man everywhere she goes, then it would still only be a matter of time before that other Brenda, the murderous one, resurfaces. We don't know what will trigger it. It will be far too dangerous to even try.

- Will they ever use her again or will they simply leave her there to rot.

- I don't know. I'll keep an eye on it from a safe distance. That's all I can do.

Soon after our plane landed in Paris.

# Elaine

It was the last day of the double sun summer. Tomorrow her side of Atraz would finally turn away from the twin suns. During the prolonged winter there would be almost no light and the thin atmosphere would be cold as ice.

Elaine was frustrated like never before.

For a very long time she had been holed up all alone inside her cave home. Her life on Atraz was a never-ending nightmare. Right now she seemed to have reached a new low. But did it really matter? Her feelings of emptiness and dread were so intense that it hardly left room for anything else.

In the end she arrived at the conclusion that she simply had to get out. Sitting inside this prison of her own making forever was not a viable option. She had to see the sun of day and feel alive, if only for a little while.

Frantically she started preparing for the outing. Even though it seemed very important, her clothes did not present the biggest problem - mostly because there wasn't very much to choose from. At her disposal she had the white high heeled shoes that dated back to the very first Grand Ball. Also she still had the famous jet blue mini skirt. The latter was in a fairly good condition, in spite of the many raves and all the late night dancing and drinking it had seen.

Rummaging through the rest of her belongings she realized that she did not have a pair of stockings to go with the mini skirt - but what the heck, outside it was still summer, wasn't it?

She had spent all night preparing the missing items. First she stitched together a couple of old handkerchiefs. The result of her efforts looked like a half decent tank top.

But then there was the matter of her hair. Way back in her heyday she had been famous for her free flowing, blond hair. Now she decided to get rid of what was left of it.

It only took a minute to cut it off. Then she moved over to the pool, but seeing her completely bald head mirrored in the water made her feel more than a little nauseous – so what to do?

Rummaging around in her small pile of personal belongings she found some twine and something that once upon a time had been used as a floor mop. Using her last good handkerchief as a base, she struggled to produce some kind of a wig. In the end the wig looked more like a hat.

It was the best she could do.

When the twin suns forced their way over the horizon and peeked into her lonely room, she was ready.

Out in the street, the good people of Atraz looked at her with disbelief.

In her worn down condition Elaine could hardly find the strength to walk down Main Street. The high heeled shoes did not make things easier. Her legs were almost as white as the shoes. The mini skirt looked like someone's sick idea of a joke, but it was the only thing about her that the denizens of Atraz were able to recognize.

To make matters worse, the upper part of her body was bent forward in an almost sickening way. It looked as if she had been taken apart and put back together again, although not very successfully.

Everything about her gave the impression that she was just about to roll over and die.

She did not have any pockets, so she did not know where to put her right hand - but the left hand was constantly busy, trying to keep the 'hat' in place.

The little girl from the Jennings household was the first to say something.

- Look mama, look at her – is that a witch?

Mrs. Jennings did not say anything at all. She took the child firmly by the hand, turned around and went the other way as fast as she could.

On wobbly legs Elaine stumbled through the only town on planet Atraz. She did not speak a single word and nobody spoke to her. They all ignored her, as if she was showing symptoms of a dangerous and maybe even contagious disease.

Back in her room, Elaine threw the awful hat in one corner. She kicked off the white shoes and sat down on the floor.

She tried hard, but she could not contain her emotions. Soon she cried like a baby.

- All this time and still I'm all alone. What can I do. Oh, what can I do?

And as the last light of the last day of summer slowly faded, she could hear Mrs. Jennings and Mrs. Trevalny discussing her predicament.

**- I just can't believe it**, said Mrs. Jennings. She used to be the one we all admired, the one we all looked up to. She was our idol, our guiding star. I never imagined that it would come to something like this ...

- It sure wasn't pretty, I will agree to that, answered Mrs. Trevalny. But we all know that she had it coming. The bigger they come, the harder they fall. That is the way of the world.

> *When I first met Yota, he was a prisoner. From the very first moment I saw him, I felt love flowing through me. Nothing but pure and beautiful love - and he felt the same way about me. I know he did, because I am extremely sensitive to things like that. But there was no way for us to be together.*
>
> *For a very long time we could not even speak a single word.*
>
> *He was a prisoner of war, an alien creature from another world, maybe the last of his kind.*
>
> *And I was the Imperial Empath. My job was to report to our military what he was thinking.*
>
> *And guess what? He was thinking of me.*
>
> *Maybe forbidden love really is the greatest love of all.*

**Next day winter came** to Atraz. Knowing that it would be a long time before her next outing, she quietly resigned to her fate and huddled up in a corner using the awful hat as a pillow. Deep down inside, her feelings played out like a nice, but very lonely love song.

> *One day they decided to move Yota out of the secured military prison and into a hospital ward.*
>
> *For the two of us that was definitely something of a turning point.*
>
> *Now I could quietly sneak in and sit by his bedside whenever I wanted.*
>
> *We were still under surveillance, but if anybody asked I would say that I was only doing my job.*

*Soon Yota understood that he did not have to say all the words out loud for me to hear them.*

*- You are not like them, he asked. Are you also from another world?*

*- No, I am from this planet. But we are of another species and there aren't many of us left. I haven't met any of my own kind for many cycles.*

*- Are you a prisoner?*

*- No, but I am not exactly free either.*

*By that time we both knew that we had to leave. But it seemed as if there was no place to go.*

*Another crucial turning point came when one day I picked up the thoughts of a high ranking military officer. Even though he was miles away from me, I had no trouble reading his thoughts.*

*He was planning the execution of Yota for the day after tomorrow.*

**As days without sunshine passed by**, Elaine was holed up inside her room. It sure would have been nice with a little more clothes to protect her from the cold that came creeping in from the outside. But the coldness of her arms and legs felt like nothing compared to the misery inside of her that she could not let go.

One of the few things a lonely empath can do, is to live in the memories – and the vast majority of Elaine's memories were of the most unpleasant kind.

*Shortly after receiving the fatal news of the imminent execution of her lover, Elaine entered Yota's hospital room. Never before had she shown Yota the full extent of her ability, but this time she took him into a private space of her own making.*

*- The day after tomorrow they are going to kill you. We have to get away now.*

*- So you want to come with me?*

*- Yes, of course.*

*- It will not be easy. I can get us out of here. But in my poor physical condition, my range is limited. If you go with*

*me, it will weigh me down and we might not be able to go far enough ...*

*- I will go with you anywhere. But we have to get out of this place now.*

*From her point of view, he dragged her into a sort of bubble floating freely on the currents of spacetime. Soon the bubble was racing along cosmic waves. Already her home planet was far behind them. To her it felt like they were moving through empty space much like a super-charged particle. She did not understand it and she did not care. She was inside Yota's bubble of love and there was no other place she would rather be.*

*But eventually he could not take them any further. They slowed down and ended up near a desolate planet with two suns. The planet itself was habitable, but it seemed to be completely empty. No life could be seen and not a sound could be heard.*

*- You have to stay here, he said to her as gently as he possibly could. I will go on and try to find a solution. Please wait here, until I return.*

After he was gone, she waited. Then she waited some more. There was nothing else to do.

She found a cave with a hot spring. She liked the water and the sounds it made. So she decided to make it her new home.

Back then the physical surroundings didn't matter much to her; she was like a fully charged battery. Leaving her home planet behind and flying through the endless space had not deprived her of any energy at all. She felt like she could go on like this forever and ever. But it was so boring and she was all alone.

**The idea had been there** all the time, but it took some time for her to surrender to the temptation. Using her power, she conjured up three young women. Soon she was having tea and eating cake with her three new friends. She knew very well that she was having a tea party with herself only. But it did not matter. She already felt much better.

So she went on and defined more women - and even men. Soon there were huge parties - and music, too.

She made up fancy dresses and new dances on the fly. It was about that time the blue mini skirt came into being.

There was, however, a certain tendency to decadence and immoral behavior. It seemed like every time she turned her back on something, situations quickly got out of hand. Therefore she decided to introduce a character who would be able to keep things on the straight and narrow.

That character was Mrs. Trevalny.

She was a stout woman who would take on any man – or woman – without the slightest hesitation. She was the keeper of morality, a champion of law and order.

Simply put, it was a stroke of genius. Soon everything went by the book.

Elaine was almost happy. Her dances became more and more extravagant. The light and the music she created were fantastic. The empty planet had turned into a place where you could easily forget yourself.

But of course, she had to overdo it. One day, when the two suns were still shining bright, she realized just how much precious energy she had spent on this extravagant feel-good adventure of her own making.

Still, she could not let it go. All of her characters stayed in place, but the level of their activities dropped to almost zero. The parties ended and the music stopped.

She had spread herself too thin - and she knew it.

Secretly she had hoped that the non-existing community of people she had created would support her in her hour of need. But when that particular hour finally arrived, those 'friendly' characters turned out to be nothing but a drain on her already waning life force. She had to give up more and more of her own personal stuff to keep the whole place from falling apart.

Inside the cave, her only protection from the cold outside was the tiny hot spring.

She no longer had the power to pretend that things were any better than they were. The lack of light and the coldness outside was unbearable. With each passing hour she longed for a miracle.

And finally it came.

A couple of days after her desperate walk down Main Street, she suddenly felt a distant light turning on. It was a very faint light, so whatever caused it would still be very far away. But she knew what it meant. Yota was coming.

More time went by and another light appeared. He was getting closer. Hope rose inside of her like an unstoppable wave. At first it only felt like little waves of ordinary optimism, but soon it was more like a tsunami of love, rushing in.

She began to prepare for his arrival.

On Main Street, Mrs. Lawson was talking to Mrs. Jennings. Like so many times before, they were talking about the need for proper clothing and what they were supposed to wear on different occasions.

- No, Mrs. Jennings said. It would be impossible for me to wear the same outfit two times in a row. Especially if we were to have a Grand Ball again ...

To her amazement, she saw her good friend Mrs. Lawson disappear right before her eyes. One second she was there and the next she was gone.

Mrs. Jennings managed to shake her head twice, then she too disappeared.

And when finally all the houses were gone – and their inhabitants too – there was only Elaine.

She was standing on a large rock, looking at the stars above. Her long, blond hair was flowing freely in the wind. The blue mini skirt looked just right and her stockings were brand new.

**Satara was in a good mood.** He was sitting in the control room, his chair leaned back and his feet firmly on the table.

- How far away are we now?
- Patience, said Matt Lauder. Patience is a virtue ...
- But not one of mine. You must know that by now, don't you?
- In reply to your original question, we have now come so far that you can take out the bait and prepare the honey trap.
- Now you're talking.

Satara was a big man. His skin was dark brown. Matt Lauder, on the other hand, was skinny and quite pale.

Satara went to get 'the bait'.

Matt Lauder could hear metal doors open and close and then the footsteps of the big man wearing his magnetic boots.

He put the bait on the table. It looked like an old fashioned, round hat box.

- What now, he asked.

Matt Lauder got up from where he was sitting. He went over to the closet with the red metal door. From the bottom drawer, he took out a round metal contraption. He placed it on the table, next to the hat box. Then he picked up the hat box and carefully placed it on top of the metal contraption. It was a perfect fit.

- This will do the trick, he said. Just wait and see.

- I sure hope we are going to catch her, Satara said. I sure hope we will.

Matt Lauder smiled viciously.

- Don't worry, he said. Just a few more hours and we will be filthy rich ...

When the spaceship landed, the two men stepped outside in their standard space suits. Out there it was pitch black. No lights could be seen. So first of all they had to set up the artificial light. Only then, and very carefully, Satara carried out the hat box with the hidden trap underneath.

Well inside the small circle of artificial light he placed the contraption on the ground. Then he stepped out of the light. Together with Matt Lauder he waited in the darkness.

- Is this what they told you to do, Satara asked. Is this enough to make her come?

- Yes. Patience, please. She will come.

And she did.

At first, her appearance seemed rather strange to them. What they saw was a tall and very thin female form slowly approaching the hat box. She did look at the men from time to time, but apparently they were of no interest to her. She seemed oddly drawn to the fatal box.

Eventually the alien female seemed to overcome any fear she might have had. She hurried over to the box and took off the lid.

Inside the box, a severed head was looking up at her. Clearly audible to the two men still hiding in the darkness, she gave off a violent scream of rage and bereavement.

Matt Lauder pressed the bottom of his remote control and the trap was activated.

For a brief moment it looked as if the ephemeral feminine form became even less solid. With great pleasure the two men saw their prey being helplessly sucked into the hidden contraption. The hat box itself seemed to be moving upwards. The alien was being sucked right into the trap.

Soon the hat box was standing on top of a glass cylinder, inside of which the empath rested peacefully, both eyes closed.

Getting the glass cylinder back into the spaceship was not an easy task. But after all the heavy lifting they felt like celebrating. So they sat down at the store room table. They could clearly see the glass cylinder and the pacified empath inside.

Quite understandably, Satara was in a good mood.

- Now we are rich, he said. We are so fucking rich. I can't believe that this is really happening. From now on we don't have to worry about a thing. This calls for a celebration. Can we have a drink now?

In the end they had more than one drink.

- I think I deserve another one, Satara said. He seemed to have some trouble getting the words right.

- OK, but this is the last one.

- Sure boss, anything you say.

Satara managed to get on his feet. He made it halfway across the room. But just as he was reaching out to pick up another bottle, there was a knock on the cargo door. He turned around and looked back at Matt Lauder, who looked slightly bewildered.

Not quite aware of what he was doing, Satara opened the door.

Outside stood Mrs. Trevalny.

Behind his back Satara could hear Matt Lauder saying: no, no, no.

Without further ado Mrs. Trevalny pushed Satara aside and entered the room.

- I have a message for you, she said.

Both men noticed that she was speaking their own language.

- Miss Elaine asks me to thank you for bringing her the head of her lover.

Looking behind him, Satara noticed that Matt Lauder had a strange, twisted look on his face that he had never seen before – and although the smaller man was now looking straight at Mrs. Trevalny, he was still saying: no, no, no ...

- Miss Elaine also wants you to know that by now she has taken possession of every little thing that goes on inside of your small and stupid heads. Therefore, the both of you are now redundant. As a gesture of her good will, she will not kill you. But she will relieve you of all your belongings, including this spaceship, and leave you here.

Satara looked at the trap. It was still there, but the glass cylinder was now completely empty.

- She also wants you to know that the only reason why Yota told you about herself and this planet was because he wanted someone like you to come here and save her. From inside your otherwise quite useless brains, Miss Elaine has learned that you come from a world called Kepi 4. She has therefore decided to pay this lovely planet a visit to see if it will be possible to find the rest of her long-lost lover. Miss Elaine wants you to know that she hopes that the time you spend on this planet will be as pleasant for you as it has been for her.

Then there was a short black-out and everything disappeared. The two men found themselves standing outside in the cold darkness.

- Where are we? I can't see a thing, Satara asked with a note of desperation in his voice.

- It's over, answered Matt Lauder. It's all over. We are doomed.

They stood there, shivering, watching their own spaceship take off without them. Soon the rocket engine could only be seen as another bright spot between the stars above.

# Happy Days on Kepi 4

Billy Brohan was on his way to Halaite. In another two hours the train would reach the port town of Talfamore. Once there he planned on boarding the sub-terra transport that would take him to the famous holiday island.

It had been a bad year for Billy. His wife had literally kicked him out of the apartment, screaming that she would never see him again, throwing his things out of the kitchen window.

Shortly after his mother died.

These events had greatly upset poor Billy and he had therefore accepted all the extra work he could get, in order to get away from his rather desperate situation at home. The military depot where he worked had responded very positively to his newfound enthusiasm for hard work.

Seven months went by and Billy had cooled off a bit. Already the world seemed like a better place and he had earned two weeks of paid vacation.

Back then nasty thoughts had a tendency to enter Billy's head without knocking on private doors or asking for permission. Every day he had to face a multitude of unpleasant thoughts and the lingering memories of dubious acts that he would gladly be without. For starters he realized that he had married for the wrong reasons. His wife was a real looker and her parents were well off. But there had been other chances, other girls. Wonder what would have happened if he had married one of those instead?

Most of all he still remembered a pretty little girl with very modest colors. Even her eyes did not seem to have any color at all.

He remembered her as a wavering, almost transparent figure with a dazzling smile. But what could have been a fond memory of a sweet girl from back in the day had long ago turned into something ominous that haunted him wherever he went.

There was nothing he could do about it. Someone told him that she had been dead for many years already. Inside of him - on the long and winding road between his head and his heart - little devils popped up, holding signs saying: "TOO LATE, PAL!"

Talking about affection and matters of the heart, one cannot compete with the dead. One typical thing is that when the bereaved remember the departed, they always remember the nice things. Another thing is that the dead never fuck up; for good reasons they never make any mistakes.

And those who are left behind will inevitably compare you to their dead partners. This might not be favorable to you, because you are very much alive and therefore perfectly able to make lots of silly mistakes.

> *So, when the train arrived at Talfamore Station, unpleasant thoughts were rolling and tumbling inside Billy Brohan's poor head. The rush to get on the elevator to the level of sub-terrain transport somehow woke him up. Entering the designated departure area, he had his papers checked. Then he was given a token. The number of the token was 87.*
>
> *When he arrived at the platform, numbers were at 73. After a short wait the sled-like shuttle with number 87 opened its pneumatic door and let him in. There was only one seat and room for his luggage.*
>
> *Sitting down he found the slot that was obviously meant for the token, which he inserted. It was duly accepted. The shuttle moved. He could feel it. A monitor in front of him came alive and started playing the latest news.*

- Today marks a sad record. For 81 periods we have not heard from Eta 3. Survivors from the last flight out of Eta 3 report widespread fighting going on between police on one hand and the armed forces on the other. Here on Kepi 4 we have no way of confirming the authenticity of these allegations. But the epicenter of the conflict seems to be the main settlement on Eta 3, the town of Shomonomu.

Billy Brohan was not eager to hear more news like that.

- Isn't it funny, he thought to himself. Here I am on my way out and already now I can imagine myself coming back again in exactly the same way, inside shuttle number 87.

He somehow felt a need to rephrase that statement:

- Here I am on my way through life and already I can imagine the day I die.

He did not say it out loud. In fact, he never said things like that out loud. Absolutely not.

**When the puny little spaceship landed** at the Kepi 4 Space Port, the customs officer met Matt Lauder, who told him that he would be heading straight home where he intended to stay for quite a while. The man in the uniform duly noted this information and left.

But instead of flying to the home of the late Matt Lauder, I flew straight to my target – the beautiful and secluded holiday island of Halaite.

By the time Mr. Special arrived, I had the whole island enthralled. Every single one of them had given up more than 60% of their life force to me and they were now waiting for the chance of delivering some more.

I spent most of my time at the shuttle station, picking up the passengers one by one. That was the most expedient procedure. The shuttle would open, I would look into the passenger, deciding which part of his or her memory I could use against them.

Love, hate or money – it did not matter to me as long as it served my purpose.

When shuttle number 87 arrived, the door opened and I saw a rather ordinary man. I immediately searched his memory for something useful and found only one thing. It was no surprise to me that it was a woman. The man in shuttle 87 was carrying around in his mind a picture of an almost transparent young girl, with hair that shone like silver and skin that was silky white. Her whole presence seemed to be very delicate, as if she was just about to disappear.

I may be sensitive, but in this case it only took me milliseconds to realize that the girl this man cared so much about was just another version of myself. Obviously we were not from the same planet, we were not of the same race, but ...

As these thoughts passed through my head, I also went ahead with my original intention of posing as her.

So when the man in shuttle number 87 looked out through the half open pneumatic door – instead of seeing me, he saw the love of his life.

I had worked my way through the memory patterns of the countless number of people, I had already enslaved.

Carefully I had scrutinized the memories of each and every person I had been in contact with ever since landing on Kepi 4.

But there and then – in the memories of the man in shuttle 87 – I found the first clue as to where Yota might be.

It was a tense moment. A strange man was looking at me, believing that he saw his long-lost love. I was looking at him, overcome with joy that I had finally found something that could lead me straight to the love of *my* life. We were both kind of dumbfounded.

So for a split second I hesitated. I lost concentration, if only momentarily.

The man in shuttle 87 looked at me differently.

- Who are you?

It was a simple question. But somehow I was not quite ready for it.

- But Billy (I now knew that his name was Billy) ...

- Don't even try to pretend. You are not her. How could you be? What do you think you are doing?

At this point I laid him to rest. I had work to do. I would have to deal with him later.

- o - 0 - o -

**I don't know what happened** to the overseer, Billy Brohan. Out of the blue I received a message that I had to come to work and do his shift instead of him. No explanation was offered.

I did not mind. I needed the money.

So there I was in the dead of night, sitting behind my desk in the dimly lit guard room. In front of me was an array of monitors, each one of them showing a room inside the Zenzen Military Depot. I was bored like never before. Luckily, somebody had left a copy of yesterday's newspaper.

The headlines were all about the blight. The reports stated that on the neighboring island of Zwitack, the disease had taken a heavy toll on the local population. Reporters had interviewed grieving family members and they all seemed to tell the same story. A sudden break-down of the normal bodily functions, followed by a seemingly permanent unconsciousness. Pictures showed victims lying still in their hospital beds. Nobody seemed to know the cause of the illness.

In the end I sighed and put down the newspaper. Even though this scourge had not yet reached our province, the newspaper articles seemed like an ominous warning.

So, I decided to do my job. I ran a perimeter test, followed by an internal sensor reading. Both tests were normal. For now, I had done my duty.

Several hours went by and nothing out of the ordinary happened.

At 4 a.m. Maria Tacka of the cleaning crew arrived at gate 21. Even though she doesn't have to, she always walks up to the guard room and gives me her usual friendly nod. Out of sheer boredom I tracked her for a little while. When she actually began cleaning the floors of Hall A18, I let it go.

Having nothing to do, I started working on my Time Schedule. I was comparing the monthly working hours I had registered to the actual sensor logs, to see if I could somehow squeeze in another hour that I could get paid for.

I was so occupied with this trivial task that I had forgotten everything about Maria Tacka until the monitor showing Hall C30 started flashing. On the monitor I had a full view of that room. Right inside the door stood what had to be the cleaning woman's abandoned cart. There was no sign of Maria Tacka, but in the middle of the room stood a tall woman in a very peculiar dress. She was trying to open a container which was very visibly labeled with a bright bio-hazard sign. She must have known what she was doing, however, because as I looked the container moved slightly upwards and the lid folded back.

Inside the container I could see the figure of a man lying flat on his back. Quite obviously he lacked his head. With both hands the strange woman now held something that looked very much like the missing head. Without further delay she put the head where it rightfully belonged.

I saw a huge spark, followed by a clear, bright light.

The figure that had been lying dormant inside the container was now standing up next to the woman. This man looked very much alive. I had a creepy feeling that he was actually looking at me.

This is where things got really strange. I tried to activate the alarm, but somehow my arm was not long enough. All I had to do was to press the big red button. But I could not get my hands near it. Every time I tried to reach out for the red button, I had a feeling that my whole perspective changed – my arms seemed to get shorter or the button was moving away from me – I could not tell. I desperately wanted to, but I never managed to activate the alarm.

The official report states that they found me the next day, sleeping at my desk instead of doing my job. At my hearing they told me that there had never been any employee by the name of Maria Tacka. When I tried to tell them about the strange woman and the flash of light and the scary man standing next to her, they told me that no such thing had happened. They said that I was simply trying to conceal the fact that I had been sleeping on the job.

- o - 0 - o -

Of all the happy moments in my life, not a single one had been better than this. Finally, I was reunited with the one and only person I loved. It did not come easy. I had to do it the hard way. I had raped the minds of thousands to learn of his whereabouts. I fed him the energy of tens of thousands to resurrect him.

It was all for love.

- Let's get out of here, he said. I don't like this planet.

- Neither do I. But where should we go?

- These people have just lost one of their planets, Eta 3 they call it. I would like to see what has happened there.

- What are we waiting for.

Once again I was flying through space inside his bubble of love. I never had the chance to tell him about Billy, who was still sitting in the tiny virtual cubicle where I left him.

When we approached Eta 3 our presence triggered an alarm. Yota made evasive maneuvers that included slowing down, going into some kind of stealth mode and plotting a new and completely different course to the planet deep below.

The natives were clearly on their toes.

We, on the other hand, were soon flying silently by without them noticing us at all.

The moment we saw them we both knew that these people had nothing to do with the humanoids back on the planet from which we had just escaped. They were not very tall and they wore a lot of garment. Their uniforms almost reached the floor. No matter how hard we tried, we could not get to see their feet. It was as if they were floating on little islands made of alien garments and uniforms.

Most of these funny people lived in an oblong crater that looked like a scar on the planet.

Apparently, they were also dangerous, because right next to the crater there was a really big mass grave. So it was obvious what had happened. These newcomers had arrived. They had killed all the humanoids and taken over the whole planet.

Simple as that.

Not a nice place.

Soon we were heading for our next destination and I told Yota why I wanted to go there.

- And you still have him?

- Yes, I could not let him go.

- Why?

- He wants me to be her. He knows that if he and I split, he will never see her again.

- So how will you handle this romantic situation?


**The object we were heading for** was actually moving away from us. So we raced past suns and nebulas until we finally caught up with it.

Long ago the Asteroid A28-40 had seen fierce battles between warring groups of humanoids. Long after the crash, the wreck of a big gunship was still lying on the asteroid.

We reused the materials from the gunship to make a dome structure. The materials from the military vessel provided a first class sealed environment.

Two power supplies were refurbished and placed as far apart as possible with the dome right in the middle.

I gently took Billy and his cocoon and placed him in the new dome structure. Then I relaxed and programmed a perfect life for Billy and his loved one that would repeat, over and over again. Every morning he would wake up to a new and wonderful day with his true love by his side. Every night he would fall asleep with the knowledge that tomorrow would be another splendid day.

I put the pieces together, started the power plants, and then I donated a little something of myself to make it real.

Soon we were leaving.

- Now he is dreaming of her?

- Yes, I can still see it from here. They are in the garden. The sun is shining. They are talking about having a baby.

- This is your baby, Yota said. You know that, don't you?

I smiled.

- You're my baby, too.

- o - 0 - o -

*Much later, the part of me that I had put into Billy's dome came back to me. Part of that transfer was something much like a log file. It revealed that after only 2,108 standard periods one of the two power plants had been taken out by a falling rock. The other lasted 230,405 standard periods before it finally malfunctioned.*

The sun was shining and Billy Brohan was lying on the lawn with his head in the lap of his true love. He did not have a single thought in his head, except the feeling that it was fine. Just fine.

And just like that his time was up, the power failed and Billy passed away.

# The Day of The Dog

I should have known that I would never get rid of him. Right from the very moment he got out of that silly spaceship I could feel him.

Later the same day he came strolling up to the house and looked me straight in the eyes.

I looked back at him, coldly.

- There are no dogs, is what I told him.

- And there ain't no cats either, he replied.

Well, touché.

# Dancing In Low Gravity

I woke up. The display on the cosmic clock beside the bed said 9 am local.

So I got up. Slipped into my brand new morning gown and went out into the kitchen. Food was on the table.

- Where are you, I said out loud.
- I'm hiding.
- Who are you hiding from?
- You.
- Why are you hiding from me. It's silly. Come on out.
- I don't want you to see me like this.
- Like what?

She appeared.

As soon as I saw her, I knew what had happened. Yesterday evening she had been a generic model only and entertained me as best she could. But while I was sleeping her AI had entered my unconscious mind and read it like an open book.

Or rater – like a detailed manual.

For some reason she had chosen the appearance of Susan V.

The very best version of Susan V. I must say - and definitely not the one that I actually lived with.

In my normal state of mind, I only had a rather blurred image of what she would look like. But my unconscious mind had been able to do a better job. A much better job.

In this incarnation she had not yet reached the tender age of 20.

Just like I remembered it from so long ago, every part of her youthful body looked fantastic. Her cute smile was topped off by her slightly red hair, flowing around her head like a regal crown of nature.

- Why can't I see you like that, I asked. You look good. Better than good. Stunning.
- But this is not what you want. I know. I have had a good look inside of you and I have seen everything there is to see.
- Everything? Really.

- Please don't play dumb. Yes, I have seen everything. This is not your heart's desire.

She emphasized the word *everything*.

This conversation made me feel like maybe this was not a good morning. I had just gotten out of bed and already I was in trouble.

- I want to please you, she said. I only want to please you as much as I possibly can. Why won't you let me put her on.

- What do you mean. I haven't prevented you from doing anything ...

I instantly regretted having said so. I knew that I could not take it back. I had already said too much.

Without any further warning, her hair began changing its color from slightly red to platinum blond. Just like that. Strangely, the color changed from the downside and up. She was also getting visibly smaller.

- Stop it, I screamed at the top of my voice. Stop it. You can't do that. You just can't do it.

It stopped.

- See, she said. This is exactly what I am talking about. You won't let me.

For a minute I breathed heavily. Not only did I have trouble breathing, I also did not know what to say.

- Please, I said. Please stay the way you are right now. If you really have seen all there is to see, you will surely know that I liked this person too.

I could not help noticing my own slip. I said 'liked' when I should have said 'loved'.

I sat down and tried to look calm and collected.

- Where is the coffee, I asked.

- o – 0 – o -

As far as I knew, the situation I found myself in was not at all my fault.

Space law stipulates that all transports of strategic ore must be accompanied by at least one bio. As the current situation clearly demonstrated, this particular law did not seem very clever. What was good about it, however, was the money. Someone like me could travel the galaxy and even get paid for it.

It was a standard procedure. When the paperwork was done, the bio who had signed up for the ride would check in at the local space station. Company staff would then guide him or her to the pod. You would be in a stasis until the huge transporter reached its destination. Then another crew would be there to wake you up. Simple as that.

Only this time when I woke up, the lid of the pod was already open. But there were no company crew members to be seen. I closed my eyes, shook my head, and opened them again.

Still nothing.

Then I heard a voice.

- This is Com speaking. I am sorry to inform you that we have engine trouble. We are approximately half way to our planned destination, but right now we are only progressing very slowly.

- Under these circumstances the regulatory framework guiding this transport requires your mobilization.

- I will now help you to get out of the pod and subsequently guide you to your quarters. There is no need for you to worry. Except for the technical problem I just mentioned, all other systems are fully operational. Our only problem is the lack of propulsion.

With some difficulty I got out of the pod. Following the directions of the seemingly omnipresent Com, I staggered down endless corridors.

After quite some time I was standing before a door.

- This is it, said the metallic voice. Inside you will find additional support as stipulated in the flight manual. Please remember that the better you integrate with the supportive interface, the more it will be able to assist you.

The door opened and I went inside.

Space travelers are known to complain endlessly about minuscule cabins, small living rooms and awkward facilities.

Not in this case.

The place was enormous.

Just about everything was standard voice controlled.

There was a big kitchen.

Next to the kitchen was a spacious living room with a huge transparent 'window' through which distant stars could be seen.

Another room was filled with odd machinery, clearly meant for bodily exercise. Moving back towards the entrance, I found the master bedroom and the toilet.

I remember wondering why the bed was a double.

- Or else it would not be big enough for the both of us, a voice said behind me.

I turned around.

Her hair was jet black and she was not very tall.

But the smile sure was pretty.

- Don't worry, she said. I am your one and only faithful supportive interface.

- What is your name?

- That is for you to decide.

- What are you?

- I am an interface, just like Com told you.

- When you say interface, I think of something else.

- Then think of me as a simulacra. A being.

- OK.

What else could I say?

- Are you hungry?

- Yes.

- Sit down and relax. I'll fix something for the both of us.

The food was excellent and there was wine. I had a lot of it. We ended up in the double bed.

Next morning she was nowhere to be seen. But her shoes were still there.

I got out of bed and found my way into the kitchen.

- Where are you?

- I'm hiding.

You know the rest.

- o – 0 – o -

Later that day I asked her:

- Am I supposed to do anything? Do I have any duties? Any chores?

- Com will take care of everything. It is not as if our spaceship is about to fall apart. You and I only use a very small fraction of the available power, so there really isn't much we can do right now except for keeping up our good manners until help comes along.

- And when will that be?

- I don't know. But it is not something you should worry about. It will happen sooner or later. Most likely a little later. But it's all right. I really don't mind.

Thinking back, I have tried to remember what we actually did that first night. Did she say something out of the ordinary? Did she simply comply with everything I asked of her?

The wine must have gone to my head. Seriously.

I woke up the next morning and had to pee. I was not all that steady, but I managed to reach the toilet and do my thing. When I came back to bed, I had a funny feeling that something had changed. Carefully not to wake her, I lifted up one corner of her blanket - and there she was.

It was no longer Susan V. lying there. It was Charlie. I could only see the platinum blond hair and her back. But I was dead sure. Charlie was lying right here. It couldn't be her, of course, because she died so many years ago.

But here and now she was lying there, breathing softly.

I felt completely powerless and sort of fell back into the bed.

This seemed to wake her up. She rolled over and smiled to me.

As always her smile was dazzling.

- Hi there, she said. Where did you go?

- I never went away. I've been right here waiting for you to wake up. It feels like I have been waiting forever.

*That's what I heard myself say.*

- I'm so glad you see things that way.

What else could I do?

I couldn't wriggle myself out of this one. I knew that. For sure.

After that our days together went by like so many heartbeats. Com had been right, surrendering to the supportive interface made everything much easier.

One night after dinner she took me to a room I had never seen before.

- This is where we dance, she said with a big smile.

- Dance?

- Yes, just hold me and set your mind free. Now we dance.

I bowed to her, she curtsied to me. We both laughed and I held her in my arms.

All the lights in the big room dimmed. From the far corner of the room came a single shaft of light, lighting up the big room faintly, as if an imaginary alien sun was about to go down.

Then it began to snow.

It was like magic. I had never seen anything like it.

- Here it comes she said.

Soft violins filled the room and a man's voice was heard singing with an old fashioned accent.

Somewhere, my love there will be songs to sing
Although the snow covers the hope of spring
Somewhere a hill blossoms in green and gold
And there are dreams all that your heart can hold

I never was much of a dancer. But given the low gravity and the fantastic interior I felt my body floating in mid-air. Together we glided across the floor.

You'll come to me out of the long ago
Warm as the wind soft as the kiss of snow
Till then my sweet think of me now and then
God speed my love 'til you are mine again

The music did not last forever, of course. Nothing lasts forever. The snow disappeared and the lights went back on.

But it certainly was the clou of the evening.

Later, as I lay beside her in the double bed, for the first time I made a conscious comparison between now and then.

The real Charlie had been a fragile girl. She always ended up in bad situations. She had a diagnosis. She was a mess.

The new Charlie was flawless. She was always there. She always told me that she loved me. How could I not love her?

- I know you do. And I love you too, I heard her say.

Always be very careful when your girlfriend can read your mind.

But I did not have to hide anything. Being with her, I felt that I was in the one and only right place. It was me and her – and nothing else. I did not want anything else. I did not need anything else. This was Heaven.

**We all know that** good things don't last. Only this time I wanted it so very much that I really allowed myself to indulge in this paradise-like fantasy. Normally fate is hard and throws all kinds of pain and anguish your way. So if for once you get what you actually want, then perhaps someone like me can be forgiven for letting it all hang out, accepting illusion rather than reality.

One day when we were sitting peacefully in the big living room it all came to an end. Without any warning there was a huge bang and something smashed through the big panorama window. A whole section of unknown origin pushed its way into the spacious room. Then all the lights went out.

The big thing that had entered the room was a semi-transparent module. It seemed to fit perfectly in size. The part of it that was now inside gave off a bluish glare. Inside of this module I saw men in spacesuits. A doorway opened on the side of the module and people entered the room. One of them came straight for me and grabbed me by the arm. The rest of them opened a door and disappeared into the belly of the transporter.

Minutes later I was being pushed through a hatch and into a small shuttle that shortly after was heading for a nearby spaceship. Not quite as impressive as the transporter, but still quite a large vessel.

Our ride from one spaceship to the other did not take very long and all the while I was looking back at the transporter, feeling a greater loss than I had ever experienced before.

When the shuttle reached its destination, I was hurried into the newly arrived spaceship. As I exited, more crew members entered the shuttle, bringing with them what was unmistakably a pod. So I was being replaced. That was very obvious.

An elderly man in an officer's uniform was there to meet me. He smiled reassuringly and led me to a room. I noticed right away that this was a normal spaceship. The rooms and the hallways were small - and I felt very small too.

Shortly after when we were both seated inside their interrogation room (what else could it be) the officer again smiled reassuringly at me.

- They were good to you, weren't they?

- Yes, I guess they were ...

- But this is it: the transporter has not moved for quite some time. It wasn't doing its job any more. It was just throwing itself a party in mid-space. So we have to get it moving. That is our job. The job we are doing right now.

- And where do I fit into all of this?

He looked at me in an odd way.

- I will let you in on a little secret. We rely on the fact that the transporters do their job. They are huge and very powerful machines. Contrary to older models, their load is now on the outside. Except for a very few places all of the finer things are on the inside, well protected by the load. You can throw a nuke at it and at best you will scratch the load. The transporter will just keep moving. The AI that guides it is very sophisticated. It has to be, because it must be able to handle a lot of difficult problems. They even have Stingers. The only way we can come near them is to broadcast certain identifying signals.

He leaned over the table and looked me straight in the eyes.

- This is the thing; they have a personality - and the real reason why there has to be a bio on board is that we need them to feel a responsibility for something – or someone. Otherwise, they might start doing whatever they please. And the transporters will cease to transport. Not good, if you ask me.

I did not know what to say.

He sort of looked down before continuing.

- We have a bit of a problem with this one. Normally we would restart the whole machinery, AI and all, and that would be it. But this one is an older model. All of its flight data and all operational programs are stored together with the – how can I say it – the more personal data. So if we provoke a full restart, we will also have to re-program the whole flight schedule and how to do this and how to do that etc etc. It would take forever.

- So right now, our people is over there doing a very delicate job. When they return, we will take you to the nearest friendly planet. You will be paid in full, plus a compensation. Don't worry, you will be fine.

- Why the compensation, I asked.

- Because your intergalactic days are over. Knowing all of this, you will no longer be eligible for bio duty.

**The planet I ended up on** was called Kepi 4. It was way out in the sticks. Maybe the company ship that brought me there was the biggest spaceship they had ever encountered.

Kepi 4 was part of an 'empire'. Honestly, that is what they called it!

When I arrived, this so-called empire was somewhat shaken by the recent loss of a planet. They did not know how or why it was lost. They only knew that suddenly all communication had ceased.

The whole atmosphere of Kepi 4 was incensed with anger and fear.

And there I was. A stranger telling a not very coherent story, sent there by a hitherto unknown organization, and arriving in a huge spaceship. What was my purpose? Maybe I was some kind of spy?

So they prodded me here and there and everywhere. They scanned me. At one point they wanted to pull out one of my teeth. Luckily for me they decided against it. In the end the only thing that saved me was the fact that I had money. The salary from my last voyage plus the 'compensation' amounted to quite a lot.

But I was stranded.

There was no intergalactic traffic in or out of Kepi 4. Having seen the locally produced, rocket-powered vessels they did have, I decided it was probably best to stay on terra firma.

Other than that I did not have any immediate problems. Many aspects of the planet itself was OK and prices for food and lodging were reasonable.

But during the long days I was so bored - and each and every night I dreamed of Charlie.

There are various kinds of bad dreams. Repetitive dreams where you are stuck inside of some kind of transportation and you have no control of where you are going would indicate that you have lost control of your life. Or you may dream of something really unpleasant and frightening and wake up shaking with fear.

Me, I have always thought that the worst kind of nightmare is when the dream is way better than reality - and you wake up cursing your bad luck that it was only a dream.

That is how I dreamed of Charlie.

And I wasn't even dreaming of the real Charlie. Oh no, I was back on the transporter being kissed and caressed by her alter ego, the lookalike.

In the neighborhood people knew who I was. Most of them disliked me, only because I was an outsider. But the one thing they all wanted was my money.

So in theory I could easily find a local woman and marry her.

But still, I kept dreaming of Charlie.

I was trapped in this stupid reality. I could not escape from Kepi 4 and by now one Charlie was dead and the other one would be light years away.

One thing that kept coming back to me was the dance and the music that played while snow was falling around us. This planet did not have much to offer, but they did have a library. So, I went there to see if I could find a clue. At first I did not know how to go about it. But a friendly librarian referred me to a voice-controlled search engine. After having hummed into an oversize microphone for some time, it came up with a name: Lara's theme.

I was in luck. I did find the music I was looking for. This time there was no singing, but it still pleased me greatly to hear it again. The meta data was almost non-existing, but to my surprise the only entry I was able to find referenced Lara's theme to original Earth.

Just how long had that old transporter been travelling from galaxy to galaxy? If what the library source stated was true, this music was ancient beyond anything I had ever known.

I would have liked to search for information on the transporters, but I did not dare. The local authorities might see such an activity as a threat.

After a while, when I had already stayed on Kepi 4 for one full rotation, an official came to see me. After having sworn me to secrecy, he informed me that a recon mission was underway to the lost planet, Eta 3. This mission would try to ascertain what had happened and evaluate what could be done. Since nobody knew what had actually happened, the mission statement was not very well defined.

- We need someone with real hands-on experience. Someone who can understand what he sees with his own eyes. Therefore, we would like you to act as a consultant. Can you do that?

- I am not a mercenary.

- We don't expect you to act like a soldier. We just need someone who is used to being in space. But even if you are not a mercenary, you will be paid.

What can I say.

The truth is that I was bored like Hell.

Two weeks later the rocket blasted off with a deafening sound. Soon Kepi 4 was but a small round thing far behind us.

When we arrived at Eta 3 things happened very quickly.

The pilot went straight for what had been the biggest settlement on the planet. I did my best to make some sense of what I saw. Several crew members were looking out through the same optical device that I was using.

The settlement was situated in an oblong crater near the planet's equator. It was only in our sight for less than a minute. To me everything seemed normal, but I could hear my fellow crew members talking about the foreign technology that could be seen down there in the streets and the buildings that were missing.

The plan was to go round one more time and look at it again.

Unfortunately, we had not taken the readiness of the enemy into account. As soon as we had cleared the crater, we were attacked. An unseen battery fired from behind us and some kind of beam weapon took out our main engine.

Our primitive spaceship made it a short distance on auxiliary power, then the pilot had to bring it down. Most of all it was a crash landing.

We hurried out of the wreck. The rest of my party were all professional soldiers, so they brought only one thing to the party; their weapons. Someone handed me a long gun. Then we ran for cover.

At that point I believed that I would die. The enemy was out there, machines were already hovering above the wreckage of our ship. To my horror another low flying enemy appeared from behind us. If they opened fire with heavy weapons, it would be fatal.

As I crouched behind some rocks, seeking shelter as best I could, I heard the one thing I never would have expected to hear in this place. Somewhere someone was playing Lara's theme.

I looked up and saw five triangular shapes diving down towards us.

- Stingers, I thought. But how ...

Two Singers took out the enemies in front of us, two others did away with the flying menace that lurked behind us. The last Stinger landed right next to me and a hatch opened.

- This is Com. Get in.

He did not have to say that twice.

Inside there were no visuals, but I could feel the stinger going straight up. I felt bad about the rest of my companions. Obviously, they did not stand a chance. But there was nothing I could do for them. After a while I fell asleep.

For the first time in a long, long time I slept peacefully.

- o – 0 – o -

When the hatch finally opened, I crawled sideways out of the Stinger.

She literally threw her arms around me.

- I never thought I would see you again, I said.

She looked up at me.

- We had a tracker on you.

- What?

- We don't leave anything to chance.

- That can't be. The morons down on that stupid planet searched me everywhere.

I emphasized *everywhere*.

- If there really is a tracker in my body, even they would surely have found it.

- You underestimate us, she said. The tracker is not in your body, my dear. It's in your mind.

# A Twist of Fate

MasRa helped me out of the pod. It was a good thing. I could hardly stand up.

- Are you OK? We will soon arrive at my home planet.

I must have looked kind of frightened.

- There is nothing to be afraid of. I won't let you down.

So, she placed me near a window. Also I had a monitor showing me various views of the surrounding.

There was a planet coming up. It was still a small sphere in the far distance.

- That is our main planet, Zentra.

- Oh.

- You might have to wear a protective mask when we are out in the open. But the rest should be OK. Gravity will be just fine for you.

I could hear that she was trying to smooth things over.

Soon she was busy with the landing and docking procedures.

I simply sat there. Logic told me that I should be afraid.

But I only felt dead inside.

I did not understand the language she used to identify herself to what must have been the customs authorities. But the activity she caused made a certain impression on me. She was not just a regular somebody coming in. That was for certain.

By now the planet had grown big. Soon there were ships.

And it was only then that I finally understood.

These were the ships I had been fighting all of my life.

How could I have been so naive.

My wife would never have walked into a trap like this.

Those were my feelings as we arrived at Zentra, the planet of my doom.